FA
Ch

Book Cover Design by Pixel86

Photography by Chloe Gosiewski

Dedication

In loving memory of
Peta Errol Searle

For your inspiration and kindness.

"I'll see you again and I will hold you close.
I'll tell you everything you missed, I
promise this.

And in the dark days, I will follow your
light, into the fields of gold.

That is where we will sit together,
forever."

Prologue

I grew up believing that all things magical and mythical were enchanting and wonderful. Take fairies for example; my mother used to tell me stories like...

'Once Upon a Time there was a beautiful, friendly fairy who lived in an enchanted world.'

Dreams do come true, just sometimes not in the way you may have hoped for. I am now 18 years old and know differently. I know that once upon a time there was a fairy; yes, she was beautiful and magical, but she sure as hell wasn't friendly.

I am Lauren Fisher and this my story, or should that be nightmare? Started last summer when my mum Nicole, and her new husband Dale, won a competition to sail around the world. She told me she wanted to see the world before it's too late. I thought it was funny that she had never mentioned this desire to travel before, or that she or Dale had even entered a contest like this, but my mother lives in what I like to call, The COLB: The Crazy Old Lady Bubble.

"But it will be ok" mum said, tossing her huge waves of curly blonde hair away from her face, "Aunt Jennifer will look after you while we are gone."

Unfortunately, my mum is very unpredictable and completely extravagant; for instance, seven months ago she announced she was heading to a ranch in New Hamlins to meet a guy she had met through an online dating website. She returned two weeks later with a ring on her engagement finger; and then a week after her return, I was introduced to my new step dad, Dale Parks.

Dale is a nice guy, but he's not what my beautiful mum usually looks for in a man. I am not being biased, the boys at school would often call her the yummy mummy. As much as I hated to hear it, she is a hot mum and very flirtatious by nature. Dale though, he was quite short and grubby looking and although she would describe him as 'rugged' he is in fact, quite simply in need of a good bath! Never the less, she was happy and it meant that she was too busy wrapped up in her own life to meddle in mine.

My life was great; well the fact I was dating Bray Simmonds, the hottest guy ever, was great. I had a job as a waitress in a café on Burton Street in the town of Middle Keynes. The job itself wasn't exactly my dream job but Bray worked there too so it meant I got to be with him all day. I never did know what Bray saw in me; I wouldn't class myself as ugly, but there were girls a lot prettier than me in town. Girls that were not so giant like. I am 5ft 11 with extra-long curly blonde hair which I inherited from my mother; hair that is completely unmanageable and utterly untameable.

One thing I will credit myself with are my ocean blue eyes, something my mum tells me I have inherited from my father; I wouldn't know as I have never met him and know very little about him. I have always asked questions about him like, who is he? What does he look like? What was he like?

But mum's response is always the same "well he's just like any other man honey" or "you know it was so long ago and so much has happened..."

Sometimes I wonder if she had actually met him at all!

I lived a simple life in Middle Keynes; the town had a population of 47,000. I had lots of friends and spent my Saturday nights hanging out at the Legends Grill, a hot spot for the young, cool people. My simple life turned upside down, all because of some chance win in a competition... or was it chance? So here it is, my story, my life, my fairy tale...

CHAPTER ONE

Lauren woke abruptly to the sounds of excited screams. It was 8.30 on a Saturday morning; she hopped out of bed just as quick as she had woken, shoving her masses of blonde hair into a messy bun on the top of her head. As she approached the hallway, she realised the screams seemed to be coming from her mother who was downstairs. Still half asleep, Lauren made her way down the spiral staircase to find out what on earth could be so exciting that it woke her up this early on a Saturday morning. As she made her way through the kitchen door, her mother, upon seeing Lauren, let out another screech. She ran towards Lauren with her arms flapping and flung them around her daughter's neck.

"Oh baby, it's so exciting" her mum said excitedly.

"We won, me and Dale won."

This was too much for Lauren to take in straight away; after all she had just woken from a perfect dream. A dream that involved her and Bray Simmonds getting married. Bray was Lauren's boyfriend. They had been dating for three months, which if you asked her, Lauren would tell you were the best three months of her life. Lauren was always one for getting ahead of herself. The way she saw it was if she were to be a good girlfriend and do anything and everything to keep him happy, he would surely marry her and they would live happily ever after.

However, Lauren was blinkered by lust and had no idea that Bray also had many other girlfriends and that her happy ever after would be just a dream.

"What have you won?" Lauren mumbled as she walked towards the fridge rubbing her eyes. Laurens mum, Nicole, was a bit eccentric and tried her very best to stay youthful and fun. Lauren could never understand why she was more responsible than her mother; she loved her mum dearly and had a good relationship with Dale but deep down she longed for her father and for the chance to have him in her life; unfortunately, no-one knew where he was and the only information she had was his first name – Zenon.

She had gone down every avenue trying to find him but no such name existed anywhere.

"It's an around the world trip; isn't it amazing?" gasped Nicole, jumping around on the spot. Lauren turned towards her mother, looking at her with a confused expression she asked, "how?"

Neither Nicole nor Dale had any recollection of entering any competition, although this didn't surprise anyone as everyone knew they were both computer illiterate with no idea what they are tapping into on the internet. It took Lauren a moment to get her sleepy head around what her mother had just said, but when she finally did she smiled, that sympathetic yet warming smile, which she gave her mum regularly.

"Without sounding like a kill joy" Lauren said sheepishly, are you sure this isn't one of those scams?

"No honey, look." Her mum grabbed two tickets from the breakfast bar.

"It's real, we fly to an island called Roatan and pick up the boat there! It's really real!"

Lauren took the tickets and examined them; surprisingly they were genuine. It took another hour or so for the screaming and flapping to calm down by which time Lauren had gone back to bed. She was happy for her mum, she really was, but the high-pitched voices and sudden outbursts of screaming were just too much for her. She figured if she left it a while the excitement might calm down.

Eventually, Lauren wandered back downstairs and asked her mum and Dale the question that had been bugging her since she heard the news; "do you intend to leave me alone whilst you're travelling or will I be coming with you?" Lauren was hoping she could stay behind; after all, she had no desire to travel the world unless she was doing it with Bray. In fact - ideally, with Nicole and Dale off travelling the world, Lauren imagined Bray moving in with her.

How perfect, she thought, we could be together all the time. Her mother and Dale's faces turned from grinning Cheshire cats to utter confusion.

"Well honey," her mother said, "I hadn't even thought about that."

Lauren rolled her eyes, she wasn't surprised.

Nicole thought for a moment, and then clapping her hands announced…

"You will go and stay with your Aunt Jen!"

Jen was Nicole's younger sister who still lived in Eden, the small town in which they had grown up. Eden was five hundred miles away from Middle Keynes and was situated deep within miles and miles of woodland. It had a population of eight hundred and eighty-seven. The small community had its own grocery store, local ale bar, salon and a church and was concealed, 10 miles off the main road; locals called it the 'Hidden Valley.'

Lauren had never been to Aunt Jens house; in fact, she hadn't even seen her for the last four years. She vaguely recalled Jen coming to their house one Christmas, but other than that it was only phone calls and emails.

Nicole had left Eden when she was eighteen and had not been back or spoken of her life there since. Nicole and Jen's parents had died in a car accident when Nicole was seventeen; she hadn't even had the chance to tell them that she was expecting Lauren. Jen was only twelve when they lost their parents; she was adopted by a family that lived 30 miles away from Eden and then when Jen divorced her husband nine years ago, she moved back to Eden and has been there ever since.

This was without doubt; the worst news Lauren could have been given. After several hours of heated discussions, Lauren finally accepted her fate. She was moving to Eden, end of story. Lauren wasn't the kind of girl who would rebel and do something crazy like, runaway. Lauren was smart and kind, but that did not change the fact that she was completely devastated. As if leaving Bray and her friends wasn't bad enough, she also had to move to a whole new town where she knew no-one apart from her aunt. As she spent the afternoon sulking in her room, she thought about a story Aunt Jen had told her when she visited for Christmas.

'Eden is a magical place' she would say, 'but magic doesn't always mean good.'

Legend had it that Fey Forest was home to an ancient evil entity; those who entered the forest were rarely seen again. The stories were so terrible that even to this day, locals would not venture across the lake into the forest.

Even though the forest had a bad reputation, from a distance it was actually very beautiful. It sat like an island in the middle of a big lake, but regardless of its beauty, the fear of the legend had the people who lived around it too frightened to venture in and, until recently, nothing had ventured out. The move was terrible news for Lauren. She felt like her life was over. What she didn't know was it was only just beginning.

Nicole and Dale were due to leave for their trip in just one week.

"One week!" Lauren shouted.

She was dreading telling Bray that she was leaving and one week was all she had left with him; she must make every last moment count. That evening, Lauren met up with Bray at the Legends Grill Bar; she walked through the doors and there he was standing against the Juke Box in the corner of the bar, surrounded by a big group of people.

As the most popular guy in the town, all the guys wanted to be him whilst all the girls wanted to be with him. Lauren always felt like she was lucky he chose her, when in actual fact, she was too good for him and his wandering eye.

Bray was 5ft 8 with a muscular build; he had floppy mousy brown hair which he regularly brushed away from his eyes. The thing Lauren loved most about him was his dark green eyes; he always gave her this lingering, smouldering look, a look which made all the girls swoon. A fact Bray knew only too well and he took great pleasure in giving that look to all the girls too. No one can deny his good looks, he was a handsome guy, and boy did he know it, but he wasn't a very nice person. He would often insult people and use them to his advantage. Lauren couldn't, or wouldn't, see this side of him, she loved him and in her eyes, he loved her and could do no wrong.

After spending the first two hours sharing him with friends, she finally managed to pull him aside.

"I have some bad news" she said whilst fighting back the tears. To her, this was absolutely heart breaking. She told him all about the competition and how she was being forced to move to Eden, but that she loved him and that she would remain faithful to him whilst she was gone and that as soon as her mum and Dale were back, she would return to Middle Keynes and that everything would return to normal.

Lauren did not expect Brays reaction to be what it was; after all he was her one true love and she was his. She had imagined watching his heart break just as hers did but instead he looked at her with a blank expression and said simply "it's over."

Clearly, she had misunderstood him.

"What do you mean?" she said, panicking that she had actually heard right.

"I said it's over. You didn't honestly think I would wait around for you, did you?"

This was a cruel blow to her; of course, she had thought he would wait for her. He was her boyfriend; only last night he had told her he loved her and that they should take their relationship to the next level. Now Bray was laughing in her face. The flock of so called friends stood around the couple and they too chuckled at Lauren, like she was some poor pathetic little sparrow that couldn't fly. Today was, without a doubt, the worst day of Lauren's life. Devastated by what he had said, she threw her drink in his face and stormed out. She was only a few feet from the door when she burst into tears.

Lauren spent the rest of her days at home alone. Everyone she knew seemed to carry on with their business with no concern that she was leaving. The girls she had gone to school with were all so consumed with their boyfriends or jobs that they barely spoke to Lauren anymore and with her building her life around Bray, she too had neglected them. The day after Bray ended their relationship, he updated his Facebook status to, 'in a relationship with Kerry Shaw.'

Kerry Shaw was Lauren's archenemy; they had hated each other for years. Once upon a time, they had been the best of friends but somewhere down the line the friendship had turned to rivalry.

Kerry was the opposite of Lauren; whereas Lauren was very tall with long curly blonde hair, Kerry was only 5ft 3 with dead straight, dark brown hair and brown eyes which were small in size. Lauren and Kerry used to be inseparable, they did everything together but Kerry's father was a drunk; he was violent and mean and would often beat Kerry and her mother.

One day he grabbed Kerry by her hair and dragged her across the floor in front of

Lauren. Kerry was so embarrassed by the incident and knowing her friend had seen this terrible side of her life, she began excluding Lauren from her life, firstly by telling their friends that Lauren's real father was a criminal in jail and that's why he wasn't around.

Children can be very cruel and Lauren was ridiculed every day for some years because of this. Lauren had never retaliated by telling people about Kerry's own abusive father, if she had, her earlier years would have been much easier but she never felt the need to pass such cruelty onto her friend. Bray dating Kerry immediately after breaking it off with Lauren was like a lashing across her heart and now all she wanted to do was to leave this town. All that was left for her to do was to pack up her life and get the hell out of Middle Keynes for good.

CHAPTER TWO

The drive up to Eden was long and lonely. It took around nine and half hours in total, although it would have taken less if Lauren had a faster car - but she didn't, she drove a beat up old Beetle which could just about reach 50mph. When Nicole first told Lauren, she was buying her a Beetle for her birthday, Lauren could not contain her excitement. She had imagined a brand new shiny Beetle, a convertible in bright pink; she pictured herself driving the flashy, new car off the forecourt and it would be the best 17th Birthday present ever.

However, what she got was 1973 VW Beetle in musty yellow. No convertible, no power steering and no electric windows. It had a great big silver rack on the roof and many dents and scratches, all of which Nicole tried to assure her gave the car 'character'.

Lauren stopped at various places on the journey; she noticed the further away from Middle Keynes she got, the more and more landscape she saw. Most of the drive was through open countryside, it was a beautiful day and the views where pretty impressive. As the day went on and evening began to fall Lauren started to regret leaving Middle Keynes so late in the day. She was supposed to leave early in the morning but she thought instead she would spend most of the morning and lunch time trying to convince her mum not to leave; this was of course a complete waste of time and now darkness was setting in and Lauren still had not reached Eden.

When she finally arrived, it was pretty much bumpy dirt tracks for a good eight miles. There were trees everywhere; nothing but trees, just as Lauren imagined. Street lights? There weren't any. The road was a long stretch of mud surrounded by complete darkness; Lauren couldn't see anything around her, so she couldn't get a proper feel for the place, only that it was creepy out there.

It felt different, almost like another world.

Lauren had wound all her windows up and pushed the locks down on the doors. Better to be safe than sorry, she thought as she leaned over the passenger seat to lock the other side. The track through woods into the village of Eden seemed to take forever, eerie darkness wrapped itself around the car, and if Lauren wasn't sure about Eden before, then she definitely wasn't now.

She soon came to an opening where the trees stopped and lights could be seen.

The village was surrounded by miles of woodland and was almost shaped like a figure of eight. There was only one road in and out of Eden and on the far side of the village was a big lake, which made up the top half of the eight. Jen lived close to the lake in an old stone cottage. Through the darkness Lauren could just about make out the beautiful lilac Wisteria plant which covered one half of the building. It had a thatched roof and white window shutters and surrounding it was a matching white picket fence. To access the cottage, you had to take a narrow dirt track off the main dirt track road. Obviously, the people of Eden hadn't discovered tarmac yet! Lauren was in a sassy mood by now.

On the left of Jens place was The Harvey Farm and to the right was the lake and in the middle of the lake sat Fey Forest, which according to the stories, had demoted angels living amongst the woodland. Lauren felt these stories were an invitation for her to explore; after all she didn't care for stupid local legends, and she had no fear of ghost stories and the bogey man.

The cottage had a large rear garden which backed onto the woods. The Harvey farm next door was not a real farm, it was a big farm house with a big barn; however, there were no animals and the owners didn't use the land for any other reason, but to live. They were Jens nearest neighbour. The Harvey family owned quite a lot of the surrounding land, but they allowed Jen to use one of their fields to home her horses. Lauren pulled up outside the cottage and turned the engine off. She sat for a moment staring at the front door; she thought about Bray and how quickly her life with him had changed to this.

The front door of the cottage opened and Aunt Jen appeared waving her hand with a beaming smile on her face. Lauren got out of the car and walked towards her; Jen had now come outside down the path to greet her.

"Come in honey, you must be shattered."

Aunt Jen put her arm around Lauren and led her into the cottage. Lauren walked through the front door and was greeted by a huge mirror hanging on the wall directly in front of her; the image of herself made her jump, she was not expecting to see the reflection of her tired, miserable self to be staring back at her. The cottage was very much like a wooden cabin inside, there were wooden beams across the ceilings and walls, and there was a strong wood smell throughout.

"You have got to be joking;"

Lauren said aloud, "I am being made to sleep in a shed!"

Aunt Jen laughed, "Don't knock it until you've tried it kiddo." Lauren was tired and unamused; let's just get it over with, she thought to herself.

The cottage was not as small as Lauren had first thought; it actually went quite far back, and it had stairs. Granted, there was only one bedroom up there, but still never before had she seen a shed with stairs. The cottage was open plan with a separate bathroom and another separate bedroom downstairs. Aunt Jen was never one for luxury items or the latest technology; the living area had a sofa, coffee table and a small TV – "from the Stone Age?"

Lauren teased as she pointed to it. Aunt Jen smiled with one eyebrow raised, "let's hit the sack, I'll give you a guided tour of the Hidden Valley tomorrow morning; you can take the room upstairs."

The Hidden Valley was what all the locals called Eden and the land surrounding it. Lauren assumed that the fact that Eden was hidden away from the rest of the 21st Century was the reason for the nickname, but she didn't feel like questioning it tonight and surprisingly, she was all out of sarcastic wit.

Lauren and Jen chatted downstairs over a cup of tea; whilst Jen sympathised with Lauren, and was pleased to have her stay, she didn't think it was fair on poor Lauren. The pair decided to call it a night and start afresh in the morning.

The stairs up to her bedroom where steep and narrow and as she opened the door to her new bedroom she was hit by the strong wood smell that emanated through the rest of the cottage. It was a very basic room; it had a large bed, a wardrobe, a small chest of drawers and a dressing table, all made of wood, and all matched the walls and floors.

Lauren had left all her luggage in the car; she was too tired to worry about bringing it in tonight, so she flopped on the bed, fully clothed and fell asleep almost immediately.

She couldn't remember having any inspirational dream or anything, but the next morning she awoke with a whole new attitude, "if I'm going to be here, I may as well make the most of it"

She sighed as she stood looking at herself in the mirror. Her massive curly blonde hair was wilder than usual this morning, but instead of tying it in a hair band like she normally did, she left it, wild and free. As she opened the bedroom door, she was greeted by the aroma of bacon and eggs. Aunt Jen looked like she had been up for hours.

"Hey sleepy head, how'd you sleep?"

Lauren smiled and replied, "Surprisingly good thanks Aunt Jen, something smells good."

Aunt Jen half turned her head towards Lauren, "I hope you're hungry; I got a bit carried away!"

As Lauren approached the dinner table she gasped, a bit? Now that's an understatement! There was enough food there to feed an army; pancakes, waffles, bacon, eggs, cereal, the works. Surprisingly Lauren managed to eat more than both she and Aunt Jen initially thought. She was now officially stuffed.

"Lauren, Mrs Taylor from the farm outside Eden called this morning. She is having trouble with her horses and I said I would help, do you mind?"

Jen had her own business caring for other people's livestock, and she also offered riding lessons and training.

"Of course, not."

Lauren sat back in her chair examining her now bloated stomach.

"I know I said I'd give you a tour and I promise tomorrow I will".

Aunt Jen was buzzing around in an apologetic manner.

"It's cool Aunt Jen", Lauren was genuinely ok about it, "I'll go out for a wander around the cottage, explore the fields, a new adventure."

Her tone was slightly sarcastic.

As soon as Jen left, Lauren had a snoop around the cottage before heading to the bathroom to get ready. After showering, she changed into a pair of light blue denim shorts and a white vest top accompanied by a pair of white plimsolls.

Lauren stood at the front door gazing out, it wasn't as bad as she first thought, the view was pretty stunning, a far cry away from the previous night's eerie atmosphere. It was a beautiful sunny morning and Lauren was feeling excited to see her new home. The village square consisted of red brick houses, a café which also acted as the village bar, a small hotel, some tiny boutiques and the village convenience store.

Aunt Jen's place was further into the countryside from the village; it had taken Lauren around 20 minutes to walk there. She noticed that she didn't see anyone at all until she reached the town square. As she wandered through the town she noticed it was quite a busy, little village and that people were staring at her. Eden was a very small community, everyone knew everyone so Lauren's arrival had set tongues wagging and had caused quite a stir. She sat on a bench outside the church for half an hour just watching the locals go about their business. She noticed that Eden did not have a school and wondered why nobody had ever thought to build one here before. Surely there must be enough children in the area to require one and the nearest town is a long way away.

On her return back to the cottage, Lauren decided not to walk back the way she came, but to instead cut through the woods. Aunt Jens cottage was situated on the outskirts of the woods, so Lauren assumed this could be a great shortcut back. She took the path through the trees, and as she walked along the path she had a feeling of complete awe; she could hear nothing but the birds singing and the rustling of rabbits and squirrels making their way through the sea of bluebells which covered the ground around the trees. From the outside, this woodland looked so unwelcoming, yet inside it was like a whole new world, like paradise.

Lauren looked up at the trees; they seemed to reach the top of the sky. This place was beautiful and serene and the aroma of bluebells mixed with mud and unpolluted air was refreshing. Lauren heard a noise above her head which startled her. She looked up and high in the sky, soaring through the air, was a huge eagle. Lauren had never seen an eagle before.

She began to fumble in her pocket looking for her phone so that she could take a picture but her shorts were quite tight and she struggled to pull it out fast enough; as she finally managed to pull her phone out of her pocket, it slipped out of her hand and flew across the ground and looking up, to her dismay, she saw the eagle had flown away.

Lauren let out a big sigh and turned to look to see if she could spot where her phone had landed.

"Oh, my goodness" Lauren shrieked.

She could not believe her eyes, as standing directly in front of her holding her phone was a boy about her age; a boy more beautiful than the bluebells in the woods or the eagle above the trees. He literally took her breathe away, and all she could do was stand and stare into his eyes, her heart racing. His eyes were mesmerising, like two ice blue moons shining into her soul; he must have been at least 6ft 2 and had a slim but very toned build. His hair was a pale, golden shade of blonde which glistened as the sun touched it through the trees. He held out his hand, "I'm Jared and you must be new around here?" There was a moments silence before Lauren finally managed to speak.

"I'm Lauren" she whispered; clearing her throat, she continued nervously

"I'm staying with my Aunt."

Never before had a guy made her twiddle her fingers whilst talking.

"Ahh I see, you must be Jens niece from the city. I live on the farm next door to you."

His voice was like pure silk that caressed her ears as it travelled.

'I cannot believe Jen left out the part about the Harvey's having possibly the most beautiful son in the world,' Lauren thought to herself.

"Are you lost Lauren?"

There was an air of responsibility in his voice. Lauren looked around her; she had been so busy wandering around gazing up at the sky and looking through the trees that she hadn't been paying attention to where she was walking.

"You need to be careful in these woods, they can lead you astray."

He gave Lauren a cheeky smile and winked, "follow me and I will take you home".

Jared seemed genuinely concerned for her safety.

'Great,' she thought. 'Not another person who believes in the silly fairy tales about demons!'

Jared smiled at her as if he had heard her thoughts; she blushed, and then thought 'of, course he couldn't hear them, that is just absurd.'

As they walked they chatted aimlessly; Lauren told him all about her mother and the trip and how Bray had acted like a jerk. He listened patiently and sympathised with her, although he seemed pleased to hear that Bray was no longer in the picture.

'Jared must have a girlfriend or ten,' Lauren thought, 'he couldn't possibly be single looking like that!'

The pair finally reached an opening in the woods. As they walked through the gap in the trees she realised it had brought her out at the end of Jens back garden. Lauren turned to thank Jared for walking her back, but before she could say anything he said, "How about we meet up tomorrow, you can meet Jade too?"

Of course, Jade must be his girlfriend, Lauren thought, typical!

"Jade is my sister; I think you two would really hit it off."

Lauren could feel her palms getting sweaty.

"Sure" she mumbled, "that would be great."

They parted company and Lauren made her way into the cottage. She sat on the sofa and took a deep breath; looking around at the wooden walls she thought that perhaps, just maybe this place would be fun after all.

Aunt Jen and Lauren spent the evening reading silently to themselves. Lauren was relaxed, she was starting to see why Jen had such a chilled-out attitude all the time, she was also secretly hoping it would rub off onto her.

CHAPTER THREE

The next morning Lauren woke feeling nervous and excited. She had arranged to meet Jared and his sister at the old barn which was half way between her house and theirs at 10am. She had been up for hours trying to decide what to wear; she had tried on outfit after outfit but nothing seemed to feel right. Her outfit had to be impressive but casual. Jared had to look at her and think she had made an effort but not too much of an effort, because she didn't want to come off like she was trying too hard, Lauren sighed, being a woman is tough.

She eventually decided on a white casual cotton lace dress with spaghetti straps which came down just below the knee which she found in Jens wardrobe; she teamed the dress with a cute pair of plain white pumps and finished the look by dabbing a pink gloss across her lips. Lauren looked at herself in the mirror, gave a quick pout and a smile and ran downstairs; as she reached the bottom she opened the front door taking one last glance in the mirror hanging in the hall, calling goodbye to Jen as she ran out and down the path.

Jared and his sister were already there when she arrived. Wow, Lauren thought, his sister is just as stunning as he is.

She, like Lauren, was very tall and slim with gorgeous long wavy auburn hair, ivory skin and brilliant bright green eyes. The contrast between her green eyes and auburn hair made her look like a photo shopped model from a magazine. Lauren looked at the beautiful siblings in awe;

'Stepford children' she thought to herself. Jared and his sister looked at each other and smiled cheekily. It looked as though they had heard what she had said and Lauren immediately tried to recall the last 10 seconds, praying she hadn't said it out loud.

"Hi Lauren, I'm Jade Harvey."

The auburn angel spoke and what a beautiful gracious voice she had. Lauren could tell by the way Jade smiled that she would like her. It was almost as though a part of her felt an instant connection to Jade.

Jade had a kind and caring aura, which sparkled and shined.

'This place has me thinking and feeling some really strange things' Lauren thought.

She quickly pushed those thoughts to the back of her head and reached out her hand to meet Jades.

The trio set off into the woods; Jared and Jade had planned to take Lauren to the Safe Haven.

"It is a place deep in the woods only us…"

Jade paused and looked over to her brother.

"Only us Harvey's know about," Jared continued proudly.

The fact they were taking Lauren to see this place that only Harvey's knew about made her feel both special and apprehensive.

"So how come you guys are showing me this place? You don't even know me,"

Lauren had barely finished her sentence before Jade grabbed her hand and gently said "We both have a good feeling about you

Lauren, I think we are more similar than you know."

Lauren knew what she meant; she felt like they were destined to meet each other, a feeling of closeness which she hadn't ever shared with anyone, not even her own mother.

They walked mostly in silence, but not because there was any awkwardness between the new friends. In fact, the atmosphere between them was mellow, almost as if they had been the best of friends their entire life. There was something soothing about the woods, the air was clean and exceptionally quiet. You almost felt as though talking would be a rude disruption to all the living organisms which resided there.

It must have taken them at least an hour to reach the secret haven. Lauren could feel they were close, she had started to feel very warm and up ahead she could just about make out an opening in the trees. Either side of the opening were two huge rocks which were covered in moss. The rocks had obviously been there for hundreds of years; they were so big and heavy, Lauren doubted anyone would ever be able to move them.

'I wonder how they got there' she thought. Surely the perfect opening couldn't have been a coincidence?

The trees ahead were not as welcoming as the others in the woods. They looked more stern and dark, like at any minute the branches could swoop down and grab you by your ankles and throw you into the air.

Lauren then began to imagine what the trees could do to Bray Simmonds, perhaps they could throw him so far up in the air that he would never return; 'if only'- she ended that thought with a sigh.

The warmth started in her chest, it felt like a warm glow radiating from her heart. It was not a painful feeling by any means. However, as they moved closer to the rocks the warmth began to spread to her hands and feet; her finger tips and toes were burning as though they were on fire. It felt like the heat was trying to push its way out of her body.

She felt she was getting hotter the closer she got. Jared and Jade were walking a few steps ahead of her;

"Hey guys," she called after them, "do you feel that heat?"

There was strain to Lauren's voice as she found herself struggling to breathe.

She was now a mere twenty metres from the opening and the heat had finally reached her eyes. It was so bright Lauren could no longer see and had her hands up covering her face to try and shield her eyes from the light. She fell to the floor on her knees with her arms covering her head. Jared and Jade by now had rushed to her side. There was a loud ringing in Lauren's ears, a high pitched constant sound piercing through her. The last thing she heard before she lost consciousness was the voice of Jade...

"Jared, why is this happening? She is supposed to be one of us!"

Lauren awoke in a daze, and she slowly opened her eyes. At first her vision was hazy and blurred but as she continued to blink she could begin to see the outline of the trees above her. She was laying on her back looking up towards the sky. The rays of the sun shone through gaps in the trees and there was a slight breeze which made the leaves quiver; with every slight gust, the direction of the rays were adjusted allowing Lauren to see the calming blue sky which sat high above the trees.

"Lauren, are you ok?" she tilted her head to see the face of the enchanting voice. Jared, who was on his knees, leaned over her – his expression of deep concern made Laurens stomach flutter. She smiled at him and asked what happened.

"You fainted Lauren, don't you remember?" Lauren turned to see Jade who was also knelt beside her. Jade took Laurens hand, "I really need you to remember what happened." Lauren sat up, "Yes, there was a bright light that was blinding me and all of a sudden, I felt a rage of heat surge through my body, it's weird – I could have sworn the heat was coming from the opening between the rocks!? You guys felt that, too right?"

Jared and Jade looked at each other. Lauren could tell there was something the siblings weren't telling her, and she insisted the pair tell her why they were keeping something from her. Jade gave Jared a slight nod, as if to give her approval.

"Lauren", Jared began, "you're not like other people, you are…" he paused for a moment… "you are different."

Lauren felt confused, 'where is he going with this?' she thought to herself.

She had barely finished that thought when Jared said, "I will tell you where I am going with this Lauren but it's not so easy to explain."

"Wait, what"?

Lauren said aloud as she jumped up. How did he know what I was thinking? she quietly asked herself in her mind.

Jared cleared his throat and began…

"Lauren, I know what you are thinking because I can read your mind. So, can

Jade and so can every other enchanted being and supernatural creature in Eden."

Lauren stood frozen as Jared went on, "Lauren, you have no idea who you are and where you come from, which puts you in great danger now you have returned to Eden. I know this is a lot to take in but your father was one of the most powerful and influential elves our time has ever seen."

Jared was now rambling, Lauren struggled to process all this information flying out of his mouth.

"The elders regarded him as someone whose opinion was to be trusted and respected, that was until he fell in love with a human."

"My father?"

Lauren's voice shook as she spoke, "what do you know about my father?" Throwing a thought at her brother 'perhaps a more tactile approach Jared!'

Jade quickly jumped in to answer the question.

"Your father's name was Zenon Valentin. He came from a long line of well-respected elves, as close to royalty as you can get when it comes to the magic realm, I am actually, a huge fan of his."

Jade shook her head, she promised herself she wouldn't gush over Lauren's father in front of her.

"You said was."

Lauren's eye began to fill with tears, "are you saying he is dead?"

Jared stepped forward and put his hand on Laurens cheek, "we don't know. He hasn't been seen or heard from since the day...."

Jared stopped mid-sentence and looked at his sister.

"He hasn't been seen since the day he left Eden 18 years ago," Jade finished.

Lauren took several steps back and put her hand up to create a distance from the brother and sister.

"I don't believe anything you are saying," she shouted;

"Elves are not real and I don't believe in magic. You are both crazy!"

Lauren ran all the way home; the tears ran down her face like an endless waterfall. The adrenaline pumping through Laurens body, she ran all the way back to the outskirts of the woods, but she had no real recollection of where she was going or what she passed on the way. Nothing made sense; she was confused and felt more alone than ever before.

CHAPTER FOUR

Lauren reached the edge of the woods, where she could see Aunt Jen's back garden.

She stopped and wiped the tears from her eyes and thought to herself how lucky she was that she had gone the right way and made it back without getting lost!

The view from here into Jen's garden was just as beautiful as every other view she had experienced since being here in Eden. She hadn't noticed it yesterday, she was so enchanted by Jared, she never even stopped to look.

Jen had a huge oak tree at the end of the garden under which sat an old wooden bench; the bench had swirly iron arm rests on either side which ran down into legs as support.

Smiling, Lauren remembered her mother telling her the story of how her grandfather had proposed to her grandmother on that very bench, so many memories had been created in this house but she only knew about a handful of them.

Nicole had been very secretive over the years about her life in Eden. The only stories she would tell Lauren were the ones that occurred before she had met Lauren's father. Lauren, now more than ever, needed to know about her dad.

Lauren walked over to the bench and sat down; the house was situated next to the lake and the bench faced out towards the clear waters. She sat on the bench and cried for what seemed like hours but was in fact only ten minutes.

She wiped her tears from her cheeks and began to think about her own childhood and what it might have been like had her mother stayed in Eden and her father had never left. She felt empty but calmer as she gazed out across lake; in the distance, she could see Fey Forest, a small island made up of tall unwelcoming trees. Lauren spoke aloud to herself, "so, this is the home of the evil entities Aunt

Jen told me about as a kid, this is so stupid." She shook her head and looked down at the ground.

"Excuse me! It is not stupid, it is very real and you should be very afraid."

Lauren stood up and spun around, this sweet but righteous voice came from the smallest teenage person she had ever seen. Stood in front of Lauren was a girl about the same age as her except she was a mere, 4ft 5 inches tall and who was pale in complexion with violet eyes and jet-black hair that sat perfectly neat on her shoulders.

"Who are you?"

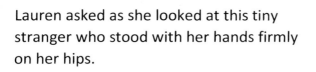
Lauren asked as she looked at this tiny stranger who stood with her hands firmly on her hips.

"Kymmie Locket" the girl said sharply.

"I am a nymph and you are a changeling."

"Excuse me, a what?"

Lauren folded her arms in an unimpressed and defensive manner.

"A changeling, half human - half magical being, or in your case half elf."

Said Kymmie.

Lauren sighed and rolled her eyes, "oh, for goodness sake, not you as well."

Kymmie stamped her foot down, "they probably already know you are here, so if you don't want to die I suggest you follow me."

And with that Kymmie swung around and stomped off into the woods.

"Who knows I'm here?"

A confused and curious Lauren hesitated for a minute, then ran into the woods after Kymmie.

For a small person, Kymmie sure marched pretty fast; Lauren had caught up her but was keeping a safe distance behind. Kymmie may well have only been 4ft 5 but she was extremely feisty and Lauren had no intention of upsetting her further. They were walking towards the woods in a direction that Lauren hadn't ventured in before; then before she knew it, they were walking through the woods alongside the lake. The dirt pathway run through the woods close to the edge of the lake, Lauren presumed the path must run all the way around the lake…

"It doesn't actually," Kymmie interrupted abruptly, "it cuts off just down there – also…," she stopped walking and turned towards Lauren, "we really need to work on you covering your thoughts. Either that or stop thinking so much it's like having a Parakeet follow me around."

Lauren was slightly taken back, mind readers, elves and nymphs – this was one heck of a crazy day and she couldn't help but feel this was all just a crazy dream and that any minute now she would wake up.

Soon the pair reached a wooden cabin. It wasn't much to look at; in fact, it looked rather shabby. The door way was bigger than a usual door would be which made the cabin look rather odd. Lauren could see the cabin was only one floor with no windows.

The wood panels were very old and had become discoloured to a patchy grey/brown. There was a porch on the front which was held up by four wooden poles that ran along the front; it was slightly slanted and looked as though it would fall down, should someone slam the front door too hard.

Lauren noticed the front door did not have a door handle and yet it looked securely shut. Kymmie marched up to the front door and simply said, "åpento" and with that the door swung open. Lauren had no idea what Kymmie had said, it sounded like an ancient foreign language. Lauren was fluent in six different languages, but this was something completely out of this lifetime. Nor did she know how what she said had made the door miraculously open, but nevertheless she followed Kymmie in regardless.

The inside of the cabin was completely empty and dark. The cabin had only one room which was dully lit by a lantern in the corner. There was not one piece of furniture, no pictures or a carpet; it was completely bare. In the middle of the room on the floor was a trap door, which again had no handle, instead it had what looked like a key hole.

Kymmie was digging in her pockets searching for what Lauren could only presume was a key. After a few minutes of searching she huffed loudly and stomped her foot repeatedly on the floor and shouted, "Jonty! That stupid gnome of yours has stolen my key again! Let me in."

The trap door opened outwards revealing a staircase under the cabin. Lauren followed Kymmie down the steps which upon closer inspection turned out to be a spiral staircase made of iron. Lauren was not sure why she was following this crazy little person down a basement in a shack in the middle of the woods, part of her honestly believed that she was dreaming. As they reached the bottom, Lauren gasped in awe. The room below the cabin was not at all what she had expected, not that she had even expected anything to be below this mouldy old wooden shack.

The basement was large with high ceilings and circular in shape. The walls were painted with beautiful maps and scripts which looked like spells. There were hundreds of candles around which filled the room with a bright warm glow. All around the room were trinkets, bottles, scrolls and various other magical looking objects. In the far corner was a very large bed. The bed was an odd shape, it was longer in length than beds generally tended to be. The bed was unmade, the red blanket was ruffled and lay in a mass in the centre of the mattress. In the middle of the room was a huge round wooden table and sat at the table was a young stocky man holding what looked like a small garden gnome which appeared to be staring straight at Lauren.

"Lauren, this is Jonty."

Kymmie made the introduction. Jonty put the gnome down and as he did so, the little man ran across the table and slid down the table leg. Lauren tried to see where he had scurried off to but was distracted by Jonty who had now stood up from the table. He was very tall, eight feet, six inches to be exact.

He had messy curly red hair, kind eyes that were an unusual shade of olive drab green. He was pale in complexion and was covered in freckles. Jonty reached forward and held out his hand to Lauren.

"Pleased to meet you, fellow changeling."

Lauren shook his hand; "We are both a changeling?" she asked hesitantly.

"A changeling is what you call a," Jonty hesitated...

"A half breed if you like, it doesn't happen often, but sometimes a being from the magic realms will mate with a human, the child is not fully magical nor fully human. Like you Lauren."

He handed Lauren an old picture; the frame was rusty and chipped in all corners. Lauren wiped the glass of dust fragments.

In the photograph stood a beautiful, young woman, Lauren knew straight away it was Nicole, her mum and she was standing with a tall and very handsome man.

"This is my mum; how did you get this?"

"That is also your father stood beside her," Jonty pointed at the frame in Lauren's now shaking hand.

"Zenon Valentin was an elf and your mother human."

"Tell me about him," Lauren pleaded as she stared down at the man she wished she knew. She was desperate for answers about her father.

"I can't give you the answers you are looking for. I never knew him and folks around here are very secretive when it comes to him. Your arrival has caused quite a stir you know."

Jonty was sympathetic to Lauren, she could tell that he would have wanted nothing more than to tell her all about him, but he just didn't have the answers for her.

"What about your parents? Are you an elf too?"

Jonty laughed, "no, I am half giant!"

"A giant?"

Lauren tried to make room in her head for yet another mythical creature's existence.

Jonty continued, his voice was soft and distressed...

"18 years ago, Eden had its very own giant called Rik; he was the only giant living in Eden. The other giants had left a few years before but Rik refused to leave as he had fallen in love. Rik would watch this beautiful woman from a distance and long to be with her. The woman was a local waitress, called Linda Stein. She had only just turned nineteen and with long chestnut brown hair and big brown button eyes she was highly sought after by many of the young men in Eden. For Rik, it was true love. He wanted nothing more than to protect her and provide for her, but being a giant, he could never get close enough to her, at the risk of not only exposing the enchanted world but also through fear of scaring the woman into never wanting to see or speak to him again. I mean, a giant at 12 foot and a human woman at 5 ft 2, it would have been the most ridiculous scenario."

Jonty bowed his head in sorrow, and Lauren could feel his angst. She knew that Rik and Linda were his parents but was keen to hear the rest of the story. She put her hand on Jonty's shoulder, "go on," she urged.

"He wasn't the most attractive male. Apart from his size, Rik was a very plain looking man, with a bald head, black bushy eyebrows and a strong jawline, but he was kind and sweet and had an overwhelming urgency to protect others, a trait that many women cannot help but fall for. The fairies knew how strongly Rik felt for Linda, and they wanted to use his despair for their own gain. So, one day they went to Rik to offer him a solution to his heart ache. They told a desperate Rik that they had a spell which would turn him into a human forever, which would allow him to be with the woman he loved. They promised him that the spell would change him and it would be eternal. You should never trust a Fairy; they are the root in which evil stems."

Jonty's words were stern.

"Rik knew the trickery fairies would wield, but he was in love and love is blind and stupid."

Jonty swung his hand across the wooden table, knocking two large metal candle holders to the ground. Lauren stepped back and turned to look for Kymmie who was on the other side of the room, rummaging through a big wooden chest, completely oblivious to what was happening. Jonty continued...

"The spell worked and Rik became human, well human size anyway. He wooed and married Linda a month after they met and soon after Linda fell pregnant.

The fairies had tricked Rik, he had not been fully changed to human, he was very much still a giant and the spell was only temporary, intended to last no more than six months and when the six months were up, Rik returned to his giant form. He retreated to woods without ever telling Linda the truth. She assumed he had left her for someone else; she was alone and carrying a baby which was twice the size of a human baby. The doctors tried everything medically possible but her body couldn't handle the stress and she died giving birth, never knowing the truth."

Although Jonty had turned away from Lauren she could still see a small tear roll down the side of his face.

His voice shaking Jonty added, "Rik could not live with the guilt and ended his own life shortly after, leaving behind their baby son, me."

Jonty stood leaned over the wooden table with his head bowed.

"The fairies killed my parents for their own amusement."

Lauren put her hand on Jonty's and gently squeezed in support of his strength.

"I am so sorry Jonty."

Lauren felt sad after hearing what Jonty had to say about how he had been orphaned as a baby. She knew the pain of not having a father but the thought of not having a mother either made her heart sink.

CHAPTER FIVE

Kymmie had now finished riffling through the chest and she slammed the lid on the chest down breaking Lauren's chain of thought.

"I got it! No thanks to that annoying gnome of yours Jonty. You need to tell him to stop hiding my key."

Kymmie was holding a long thick silver snake chain in her hand; it looked like a normal necklace, but in place of what should be a pendant was a very plain and simple long silver skeleton key. Kymmie swung the chain around the finger then quickly placed it into her jacket pocket.

Lauren found Kymmie's quirky look refreshing. You would never see anyone in Middle Keynes wearing the same attire as Kymmie. She wore a pair of black and white leggings, which had rips and frays all over the legs. On her feet, she had a pair of black and silver high top trainers. On her top half, she wore a white floaty mini top which bared her flat and toned midriff; Kymmie pulled this look off effortlessly and over the top she wore a black leather studded jacket, which like her leggings were worn and torn.

Jonty chuckled to himself, "I should warn you about my gnome Lauren; he is a mischief, a practical joker and he likes to hide things."

Out of nowhere the small gnome popped up and stood awkwardly on the wooden table.

"His name is Darrig, Darrig, this is Lauren."

The gnome blushed and hid behind Jonty's arm which was still resting on the table.

"He is shy at first but don't worry, you'll be the best of friends in no time."

Jonty was still chuckling to himself. Lauren gave a nervous smile; the gnome was an odd-looking creature, no more than ten inches in height.

His arms and legs were slim but he had a little pot belly which his yellow t-shirt struggled to cover. He had pure white hair with a beard and sideburns to match. Although he had white hair his face was young with no wrinkles.

Gnomes were pretty much extinct nowadays, they were wiped out nearly 100 years ago by the fairies who had no time for their mischievous trickery. It's estimated that there are around 80 surviving gnomes in the world with most of them in hiding. They had no magic, therefore they were unable to protect themselves from any pending danger. Jonty had always kept Darrig safe and Darrig was a loyal companion in return.

Lauren glanced down at her watch, it was 7pm!

"Oh my gosh, look at the time, I have to go!" The day had run away with Lauren and she had no idea it was so late. Aunt Jen would be pacing the room wondering where she was.

Lauren hoped that Jen hadn't rallied up a search party, that would be embarrassing and Lauren felt as though she needed no further attention to her arrival. After what she had seen and heard today, she was almost certain a nurse from a mental health institute would turn up and take her away should she actually tell Aunt Jen where she had been.

Kymmie walked Lauren back to Aunt Jens place;

"I am sorry if I came across rude earlier Lauren."

Lauren glanced over at Kymmie and for a moment she saw a look of innocence in Kymmie's face. Kymmie was tough on the outside but Lauren caught a glimpse of a sweet vulnerable girl who had no choice but to be strong. Kymmie looked at Lauren and they shared a simple smile which they both understood. They had found a mutual understanding of one another.

On the walk back, Lauren asked about how she and Jonty came to be friends.

Kymmie explained to Lauren that, nymphs are bound to a particular land form in a particular area; for example, Kymmie was born to a spring in Eden, in a part of the woods that was believed to be sacred. She is not able to leave Eden and should any harm come to the spring to which she is attached, that harm would in turn have effect on her own life. When Jonty was born he was ordered to be sent to an orphanage in Claxdyle 40 miles away, but Rik hijacked the car and stole Jonty from the humans and took him into the woods, leaving him next to the spring before taking his own life.

Although Rik had no intention of living on, through his despair and clouded vision, one thing he was sure about was that Jonty needed to be around others from the magical realm.

It was his birth right and being brought up in an orphanage by humans was not what Rik wanted for his changeling son.

Jonty was found by Kymmie's grandmother who was at the spring preparing for the birth of Kymmie. She took the baby changeling in and helped to raise him, along with the help of the elves. Although Rik had been selfish and cruel, it was agreed amongst majority of the Magical elders that they as a unit, would care for the innocent boy as his unfortunate fate was handed to him due to foul play actioned by the fairies. One thing all magical beings agreed on was that the fairies needed to be punished and their victims spared. Jonty and Kymmie were of the same age and grew up together; they were inseparable.

When Lauren reached the edge of the woods she said goodbye to Kymmie and ran back to the house. She opened the front door expecting Jen to be frantic and angry, which is how her mum Nicole would react to her being out all day in a strange place. Instead Jen was sat on the sofa engrossed in a book.

"Jen, I am so sorry if I worried you by being gone all day, I..."

Before Lauren could finish Jen put her hand up to stop Lauren from continuing.

"It's ok Lauren, I bumped into Jared earlier and he told me that you had made some new friends and were out exploring and having fun – plus it is only 7pm so you can stop worrying Cinderella."

Jen smiled and Lauren felt a wave of anxiety release from her body. Aunt Jen really was cool to live with, her laid back attitude and hippie lifestyle made Lauren feel at home. Lauren and Jen spent the rest of the evening talking about Eden and Lauren told Jen all about her new friends, leaving out the part about them being supernatural of course.

Lauren wanted to see if Jen knew anything about the so-called magic in town and had tried to drop subtle hints to see how Jen would react. Lauren was certain that Jen was oblivious. Jen didn't seem to know about anything other than horses. Lauren had hoped that Jen would know if Jared had a girlfriend or not, seeing as they lived next door, surely Jen would have seen him with someone?

But no, Jen knew nothing, she didn't even know that the hairdresser in town and the mayor had been having an affair. Lauren had been here only a few days and she already had the full scope.

Lauren decided to head up to bed around 10.30pm. Even though she was so tired, her brain just couldn't switch off. She lay on the bed trying to recap on the day's events. The day had started with her meeting a gorgeous boy and his equally beautiful sister.

Two normal people with good genes turned out to be elves? How was that even possible? Not only were they elves but they also knew of her absent father, who he too was an elf making her half elf.

Her whole life, Lauren had been searching for answers about him, maybe finally she would be able to get them?

Then of course there was Jonty and Kymmie, a gentle hearted half giant and stubborn and feisty nymph. These strange and unusual people had come into her life warning her of danger and fairies. Fancy fairies, of all things, to be something to be afraid of; as a child, Nicole would read Lauren stories about fairies.

They were described as enchanting, friendly creatures, yet now she was being informed that they were the furthest thing from friendly as you can get. As for a living gnome, Lauren was sure that at one point they had a pottery gnome in their garden and not for one second did she ever think that it represented a real thing.

Yesterday Lauren had laughed at the thought of anything make believe, magic was simply a myth that she refused to believe in.

With all this being said, Lauren still was not convinced that all of this was real.

After all she hadn't actually witnessed any real magic, all she knew was what four teenagers had told her and for all she knew they could have simply been a bunch of crazy country folk, trying to scare her.

Lauren never really got close enough to Darrig the gnome to be able to tell whether he was real or if he was some kind of electronic toy.

As Lauren closed her eyes, her final thought before falling asleep, was that one way or another, she would get the answers she was seeking.

CHAPTER SIX

BANG BANG BANG...

Lauren awoke abruptly, she sat upright, her hair was as wild as ever.

BANG BANG BANG...

Someone was at the door – trying to break it down, Lauren thought to herself. She ran downstairs in her pyjamas.

Who on earth is banging on the door like that and where is Jen? Lauren opened the door to find Jonty standing staring at her.

The banging so hard now made sense to Lauren, he probably had no idea he was hitting the door with such force – being half giant and all.

Then yesterday's events came flooding back. No — it had not been a dream, what had happened was very real.

"Hey Jonty, what are you doing here?" Lauren said whilst rubbing her eyes.

"There is much you need to know and lying in bed all day won't get you the answers you're looking for!"

Jonty clapped his hands and made Lauren jump. She looked up at the clock hanging on the wall.

"What!"

Lauren gasped it was ten past twelve in the afternoon, no wonder Jen had gone out it was lunch time, Lauren had slept for nearly fourteen hours.

Jonty insisted on waiting outside whilst Lauren got ready. She would have preferred him to come in and sit down to wait, knowing he was stood outside made Lauren feel even more rushed to get ready.

She quickly showered and threw on a pair of casual boyfriend jeans and a white tank top, leaving her hair wet to dry naturally. Lauren knew that by this afternoon she would regret doing this as it would almost definitely dry into a massive frizz and she would end up looking like a lion, but Jonty was waiting and she didn't want to keep him any longer than she already had.

When Lauren eventually went outside, she found Jonty sitting under an oak tree near the lake. It was a warm sunny day and there was a slight breeze in the air. As she approached, Jonty pointed to Fey Forest and began to tell her about fairies.

Lauren learned that there were four fairies living on that island. They were being kept on the island by a spell which the kappa had placed eighteen years ago – kappa are the water creatures, Jonty explained, they are much like Mermaids but without the fish tails. Each clan has exactly twenty-one kappa and only one clan can exist in a single water mass, except for the kappa in the seas and oceans, they are individual clans that are essentially ruled by one very powerful and very nasty group of kappa.

These kappa in Eden's water, look like humans, speak like humans and are able to walk around on land like humans, the biggest difference is they live underwater. When they are submerged in water, their skin turns a grey/blue colour and their eyes triple in size, whilst turning a fluorescent yellow. Then as soon as the air touches their skin, their appearance changes, the skin becomes tawny, the eyes shrink and they can easily be mistaken for a human. Most kappa are forbidden to walk around towns and lure humans back to the water's edge, however, there are a lot of clans which live in areas which are ungoverned by the elders and they tend to live by their own rules.

The elders only get involved if the kappa draws too much unwanted attention to a place.

For instance, a few years ago two clans in Pirot, Serbia had gone on a binge eating spree and wiped out the entire City. The Gradski Bazen Clan & The Kompenzacioni Bazen Clan united for one day and indulged to celebrate the unity.

This of course brought reporters from all over the world. They were questioning how and why every single person in a busy City had just completely vanished.

Freshwater kappa are usually the tamer breed. Salt water kappa are much more violent and unlike the Freshwaters, Salters are unable to change their appearance, which means they don't have the luxury of wandering the land, which is a good thing, because Salters are the next worse creature in the world after fairies!

Luckily for Eden, the kappa in their lake follow the laws and rarely venture out of the waters in which they settle.

"Lauren, I must warn you, the kappa are not your friend, although they seem like they are protecting the humans by keeping the fairies trapped over on the island, but they only did that because that is what the elders voted on.

The kappa feed from a human's soul. They lure people, mostly children, because the soul of a child is purer than that of an adult. The entire clan of kappa can be fed for a whole month, just from one single child, whereas an adult can only provide a week's meal for only half of them.

Once they have gotten their victim to the water's edge, they pull them in and drown them. Jonty warned Lauren to be careful when approaching the lake, you are a changeling, which means you still have a human soul, and yours is also still untainted, so they will try to take it if they get the chance."

"When was the last time they killed a human?" Lauren asked nervously.

Jonty sighed and scratched his head, before answering; "around three months ago, a group of five children were playing in the woods by the edge of the lake – one of the children got separated from the others. A kappa, lured the young boy to the water's edge and pulled him in, the people of Eden call it a tragic accident, but we all know the truth."

Lauren was horrified by what she had just heard. Surely the people of Eden should know what dangers lurked around them, it was only fair that they be given the opportunity to try and protect themselves.

"Lauren, you need to be realistic, the only way all magical creatures can live together without war, is if we all accept each other. The kappa are only able to take one soul per month if it is a child and three if they are adults. The Police Captain in Eden is a bogle, he is in charge of sacrificing souls to the kappa. As a bogle, he has the ability to get inside the minds of humans. Most bogles do this just to haunt them, it is how they get their kicks. But the chief of police here in Eden was chosen as he can see when someone has done bad things. He leaves Eden and brings back men and women who have done terrible things to others and offers them up to as a sacrifice. The bogles cannot always find someone and that's when the kappa get restless and take children. The elders made an agreement and we all should respect it. One soul is enough for survival, it is a big compromise on the kappa's part. Everyone must abide by the rules, when the fairies didn't, they were punished."

Jonty, was blunt in his explanation. Lauren could tell he didn't agree with it but had no choice but to accept it as this was just how it must be. The pair sat in silence staring out onto the water. Lauren was so shocked by what she had heard, the innocent people of Eden were living in danger, day in, day out and knew nothing about it. A tragic drowning was in fact a vicious supernatural killing? How on earth could anyone allow this?

"Hey guys!"

The silence was broken, it was Kymmie.

"What have I missed?"

Kymmie questioned as she sat down beside Lauren.

"Oh, not much," Lauren sighed, "Jonty has just been telling me about the vile creatures we have lurking in our waters."

Kymmie chuckled to herself, "well you had better be extra careful now Lauren as they are probably listening to every word you are saying."

Lauren rolled her eyes, "I guess that means that I can't go skinny dipping on Friday night, like I had planned." – Laurens tone was sarcastic and unamused. "So, what is the plan for today?" Lauren changed her tone – she tried to be more positive and upbeat. So far everything she had heard revolved around bitterness, evil and death.

Kymmie jumped up "Firstly, we need to work on you covering your thoughts, not only is it incredibly annoying but it is also very dangerous for you. All supernatural creatures can hear your thoughts, so you need to guard them accordingly." Jonty was now standing too, "Kymmie is right, Lauren all it takes is for one of your enemies to hear one weakness and they will use that against you."

"So, can the elves hear my thoughts too?"

-Yep, the duo answered in unison.

Lauren sat quietly for a moment, she had a flashback of when she first met Jared, she had thought to herself then how gorgeous he was, how blue his eyes were, ice blue moons if she recalled correctly. Lauren started to panic, 'oh god, please don't let him have heard that.' Kymmie and Jonty giggled, Lauren looked up at the pair.

"So, you have the hots for Jared."

Kymmie snorted.

"Seriously!"

Lauren was now on her feet, "get out of my head!"

It doesn't work like that Lauren, we don't have to try and enter your mind, and we don't need to do anything, it's like when you speak, our ears naturally hear your voice. Jonty put his hand on Lauren's shoulder.

"Our minds can hear your mind."

-Yeah, Kymmie added, it's not like we want to hear you rambling on about Jared's perfect butt.

Jonty nudged Kymmie.

- Ok Ok, Lauren threw her hands in the air, let's just get started, what do I have to do!

Jonty and Kymmie looked at each then turned to Lauren.

"Well, firstly, you are half elf which means you need the guidance of an elf."

Lauren sighed as she rolled her head back, so that means I need to go and see Jared?

Now Lauren was aware that Jared knew how she was thinking about him, he was the last person she wanted to see.

Lauren felt embarrassed but knew that to prevent any further embarrassment she said to bite the bullet and face him.

On the walk, over to the Harvey family's barn, Jonty filled Lauren in on how the process of covering thoughts is done.

Each supernatural creature has its own crystal or stone, sometimes they have two, in which they draw their energy from.

For example, us giants use the black obsidian, it is like our spiritual protector. The elves use Morganite; a pink beryl which is a crystal of divine love, and also Quartz for power.

An elf will sit with you every day for a few hours until you have learnt the art of covering.

Jared will be with you and connect with your mind to strengthen senses, said Kymmie.

"Does it hurt?"

Lauren nervously asked.

"Sometimes humans find it painful but majority just find it uncomfortable."

The trio arrived at the gates of the Harvey's Farm. Lauren took a deep breath and pushed the big metal field gate open.

CHAPTER SEVEN

As Lauren started walking towards the house, she turned back to see Jonty and Kymmie standing at the entrance.

"Well?"

Lauren called, "are you coming or what?"

- Sorry Lauren, this is an elf matter but we will catch up with you later.

And with that the pair turned and walked off.

"Great!"

Lauren huffed aloud, she turned back around began walking towards the house.

The Harvey family had a beautiful traditional farm house; it had grey slate roof tiles and the body of the house was made from red wood cladding.

The windows and door frames were clean and bright white. Anyone who could see, could tell you the property was well looked after; the whole building was pristine and very welcoming.

It also had a white wooden porch which wrapped itself around the house and there were five wide steps leading up to it.

As Lauren reached the final step the front door opened and there was Jared, standing tall with a big smile on his face.

Jared's blonde hair was quite long for a guy, it flopped across his face slightly exposing his gorgeous blue eyes.

Lauren noticed that his eyes were much darker today than the last time they met. His eyes were light crystal blue yesterday, but today they had a thick navy-blue ring around the edge of the iris which made his eyes appear much darker. He was still gorgeous though, she thought; crap!

He totally heard that!

Lauren was blushing, she could feel her cheeks getting hotter.

"Hi Lauren, come in."

Jared stood aside and let her walk through the door cheekily smiling as she passed.

He led her into the sitting room. The room was big and bright.

"Aside from being an elf my mother is also an interior designer."

Jared smiled and Lauren felt her knees tremble.

"Your parent's have normal jobs?" she asked.

This thought puzzled Lauren.

"They sure do, my dad is a doctor, and well, the only doctor I should say, in Eden."

Jared chuckled to himself and went on; very few of us from the magic world live a normal life, but those of us who do; have normal jobs, go to normal schools and live in normal houses, as it's the only way we will fit in with the humans.

"School!"

Lauren gasped as she remembered.

"I noticed Eden doesn't have a school, why is that?"

Jared told Lauren that with the kappa being so close to where the humans lived, they decided to move it out of town and as far away from any water as possible. The children are too vulnerable here in Eden.

Jared went on to tell Lauren about, The fairies.

They live in tree houses over in Fey forest and any man-made items they have are ones that had when they were imprisoned years ago.

"So, what is the deal with the fairies?"

Lauren hesitated for a moment, "How can tiny little pixies with wings be so much trouble?"

Jared put his hand out to Lauren offering her a seat on the sofa.

"Please take a seat."

His voice was so enchanting to Lauren, everything about him made her nervous and excited at the same time.

Jared sat down beside her. fairies are tricky creatures. They were created for the sole purpose to destroy anything and everything. There used to be three families of fairies in Eden but your father and my parents along with a few others killed two of the families eighteen years ago, so now only the Kane family remain on the island.

They were a lot stronger and much harder to kill, so instead a spell was bound to keep them imprisoned. Lauren's hand began to shake, so her father, who abandoned her, turned out to be a murderer?

Jared quickly took her hand, putting both his hands around it and held tight.

Lauren began to feel the shaking ease off so Jared continued, "Your father did what he had to do to protect you. It may not seem that way now but I can assure you, it was the only way to ensure you and your mother survived".

"What do you know about him?"

Lauren looked at Jared, searching his face for answers.

"Zenon is a big deal to elves everywhere, Jade is a big fan of his. He has protected humans for so long and he even formed, the elders Circle. I know as much about him as the history books tell us.

I can tell you about Zenon Valentin, the powerful leader.

I am afraid I do not know anything about, Zenon Valentin, the husband and father."

Jared could feel Laurens disappointment.

"My parents will be home in a few days and they will be able to tell you more. Us kids were never told very much; we were all told we would know more if the time ever came when we would need to know more."

He paused, and then gave Lauren's hand a gentle squeeze, "I think your arrival is that time, you coming to Eden seems to have gotten all the older supernatural folk jittery; even my folks took off soon as you came and were very secretive about where they were going."

Lauren sat in silence. Every day in Eden was full of shocks and surprises, she felt confused and over whelmed. Jared could hear her mind reeling through everything that had happened since she had been here.

"Lauren, let's make a start on you covering your thoughts."

He was so kind to her, everything he said and every action towards her was gentle and caring; she had never experienced anything like that before.

Bray had always been so cold towards her, sometimes ignoring her for days; in the back of her mind she knew he didn't care but she convinced herself he did and made excuses for him, like 'maybe he was busy or had no signal'. Just thinking of Bray made Lauren feel angry and upset.

Jared pulled out two small stones; one was a Quartz, which was rough on the surface and white in colour, almost like a lump of glittery chalk. The other was Morganite, peachy pink in colour and looked like a pink diamond. He asked Lauren to hold her hands out flat, palms facing upwards, and then placed the Morganite in her left hand and the Quartz in her right.

The crystals felt warm against her skin. Jared then began to talk her through the process. I will be connecting with your mind and covering your thoughts like a shield. At first it will feel strange and in some cases, can be painful. You are a strong-minded person so for you it will probably be more painful than strange but as you get used to it, those feelings will go, but I promise you I am not going to hurt you so you need to be strong and push through it.

We need to teach your mind how to cover those thoughts so that in time you will start to recognise that feeling and eventually be able to do it naturally.

"Are you ready? Take a deep breath and relax, Oh, and for the record, this Bray guy is an idiot."

Lauren laughed, and surprisingly she started to feel herself relax. She closed her eyes. As Jared placed his hands-on top of hers, she could feel her hands getting warmer and within a few minutes the warmth was spreading up her arms, through her elbows and onto her shoulders then up into her temples.

At first Lauren, didn't feel any pain; the warmth was more soothing than painful. She took deep, slow breaths, and felt relieved; this really wasn't as scary as she thought it would be.

But then, within seconds of that thought Lauren felt a sharp pain shoot through her head.

She yelped!

"Try and stay strong,"

She heard Jared's voice; she really wanted to show him she was strong and not some weak pathetic girl like Bray had always made her feel. The shooting pains were now flying through her mind like fireworks, and tears were rolling down her cheeks as she tried to push through it.

"It will go soon, it will go soon," Lauren kept telling herself this over and over but the pain was not going, if anything it was getting stronger.

"ARGH!" Lauren screamed.

CHAPTER EIGHT

Amongst the trees deep within Fey Forest, the fairies had built their home. There was no denying the architectural skill these creatures possessed. The Kane family had built homes up in the trees. These were not your normal tree house's that you might find a child playing in at the end of their back garden. These oval shaped houses were beautiful.

Made from wood, they sat up in the branches like an enormous bird house. There were four in total, all in different trees but all within a stone's throw distance of one another.

Each house came complete with a balcony made from weathered wood decking and rope. The roofs were made of bark which covered the top half and a living root bridge, connected all four houses to one another.

A clear stream ran below, through the trees. It started at the north part of the island and ran right through the middle and out on the south side. The ground was covered in Epipogium aphyllum, also known as Ghost Orchid. These flowers were nearly extinct, a saprophytic plant, obtaining its nutrients from dead organic matter. This rare flower lacked all green pigment and they had no leaves. They are an unusual flower, with them having no green colouring, they look like they are dying when they are actually in full bloom. To see an area completely covered in these incredible wild flowers was a unique and rare sight. Although enchanting, this place also had an eerie feeling. It was dark here and quiet, still and quiet.

"She is here, I can feel her."

Freja Kane was stood with her head tilted backwards, her arms slightly open, palms faced upwards as she took deep breaths. Dressed in a burnt orange chiffon dress, the boat neck design showed off her toned and slender arms and chest. The bottom of her dress swayed and tasselled, covering most of her leg, but leaving enough to show off perfect bronzed pins. She was a vision of a temptress and she played the part to perfection.

She was standing on the wooden balcony, overlooking the stream, deep amidst the trees in Fey Forest. Freja is the eldest Kane daughter and some may argue the most beautiful of fairies.

What you saw on the outside, the beauty, the charm, the innocent damsel acts, that she had perfected many moons ago; well, they were most definitely not a mirror image of what lay beneath.

Freja was tall and slim; her shiny chestnut coloured hair was long with a slight natural wave.

Freja had the clearest complexion under a few perfectly placed golden freckles and a million-dollar smile that could launch a thousand ships. Perfection she was, but the one main physical feature that had everyone who ever came into contact with her completely mesmerized were her eyes.

Freja had the most intense amber eyes; the colour was an extremely rare colour for a human, which is why most humans found them so enchanting. Gazing into her eyes was like looking into the eyes of a fierce wolf, and like a wolf, Freja had no desire to run with any other pack apart from her own.

Freja, who had been entrapped in the forest on the tiny island in the centre of Eden for the past 18 years, felt Laurens arrival like a rush of adrenaline. Physic ability was not a natural trait for a fairy to possess, but Freja had some kind of connection with Lauren.

They were born lifetimes apart but somehow there was a link between the two. Freja had the ability to see things that were happening around Lauren. A gift that only came to Freja on the day Lauren was born; but seeing as though the fairies were trapped in Fey forest with no communication to the outside world, they were not able to find out why Freja had acquired such a power. And although Freja could see Lauren in her mind and could see she was powerful and from a place far away, she did not know anything else about Lauren. Freja was not entirely sure why the link was there, nor did she know who linked them in the first place, but whatever it was, it can't have been an accident.

"Oh look, here she goes with the whole, I can feel something crap"

Amara Kane had a sarcastic tone. Freja glared at her younger sister from the corner of her eye, "Go away Mar!"

The two sisters were not as close as most siblings, in fact Amara had absolutely no time for her elder sister. She could see past the beauty in Freja and upon looking at her sister all she could see were all the horrific and cruel things that she witnessed her sister do.

Now it was true that fairies were unkind and troublesome beings, but Freja had always taken it that step too far, which is a gene she inherited from their unruly father Kais. Freja worshipped her father, he was cruel and vindictive and she wanted nothing more than be exactly like him and Amara wanted nothing more than to not be like him.

Not only did Freja and Amara act like they weren't related, they also looked completely different. Whereas Freja had long chestnut hair and eyes like balls of fire, Amara had much shorter, pearl blonde locks, which were straight as an iron.

Like her sister, Amara also had mesmerizing eyes. Amara's eyes were a stunning cool violet; she had the most unique intense stare, her eyes would almost lock on you and freeze you in your tracks. Unlike Freja, Amara would never be seen in a dress or any shade of orange. Opting for a long grey skirt and black vest top, Amara very rarely changed her choice of style or colour, not one to stand out or make a statement, she was much more reserved.

Amara also had distinctive scarring on her left cheek. Two very small oval shaped scars that were slightly raised and looked like two falling teardrops. These very small but very prominent marks were coincidently situated right were teardrops would be. It almost looked as though her tears had frozen mid fall and seeped into her skin. Amara was no angel but as far as fairy deceit went, she was actually one of the nicer fairies still in existence. Unfortunately, her father, Kais saw her more of a disappointment – he felt she let the whole Kane family down, but Amara didn't care.

With that being said, the two now had a mutual understanding. Amara had a hold over her older sister, a strong hold that was kept a secret within the family. Freja really was a piece of work; she would not listen to anyone with the one and only exception being her younger sister.

"Well, what do you expect Freja, you keep drabbling on about some girl you think you're connected too and how she will be the key to our liberation."

Amara was stood with her hands firmly on her hips; she was getting extremely distressed.

"18 years you have been talking about this girl and her powers yet here we are, still incarcerated on this stupid little island, with nothing to do, except watch Eden go about its business from a distance."

As Amara grew more and more angered, the tear shaped scars on her cheek began to turn grey. Freja quickly rushed to her sister's side.

"Mar, please don't get upset, your tears are turning, please Mar, I beg you."

Freja had her arms around her sister, trying to calm her down.

"Listen Mar, I know you don't understand, but this girl, she is here and she is the key to our salvation, you have to trust in me."

Being trapped in this forest had started to really take its toll on Amara, she had no hand in the evil scheming that had gotten them all imprisoned in the first place, and felt that she was yet again the victim of her family's malicious actions. Deep down she loved her family with all her heart, even though she did not agree with the path they had chosen.

Amara had lived in peace for many years alongside humans, elves and other mystical beings; that's not to say she hadn't done her fair share of trickery and murder, but she knew that if she played it low key life would be far sweeter.

"Amara! Freja!"

A voice shouted up to the tree house from below. It was Benny Ward, their annoying 'adopted' brother. Amara and Freja grew up with Benny and although he looked a similar age to them, he was in fact twenty years younger. Benny was not blood related to the girls, if truth be told, they didn't even know who or where he even came from, but they had never known any different, he was just always around.

Benny was just a baby when their father brought him into the family and whenever the sisters had asked their father who Benny's parents were, he would simply say he is the son of a very old friend, who he owed a favour too.

Over the years the girls got used to this fact and stopped asking, but neither Freja or Amara had ever heard of any Wards being mentioned by anyone, ever. Benny was 5ft 8" he had mousy brown hair and his physique was very strong and muscular. The kind of body human girls go crazy for, strong arms, strong shoulders, and breaking a human girl's heart was his favourite game. Like the gorgeous sisters, Benny was like a vision of a god and as he stood below the balcony in just a pair of grey chinos, his tanned and toned torso on display - he looked just like a photo shopped male model and upon closer inspection you could see his eyes, like the girls, were unique and tantalizing. Benny's eyes were an unusual mixture of greens and browns, the outer edges of the iris were a fresh bright green and as it got nearer to the pupil it became darker and darker until just around the edge of the pupils, was a warm brown ring that was tainted with flecks of gold.

"Shhh do not say anything, he might go away if we keep quiet,"

Amara whispered to her sister.

"What do you want Benny?"

Freja sighed and walked over to the balcony. Benny was standing looking up at the girls, holding a dead rabbit in the air, his facial expression was that of a man, clearly very impressed with himself.

"Who fancies Bugs Bunny burgers?"

Benny chuckled to himself - the girls were clearly unimpressed.

Amara joined Freja on the balcony, "Get that disgusting thing out of here Benny!" she shouted.

Still laughing to himself, Benny chucked the carcass up at the girls and ran away into the trees, leaving the girls screaming some choice words at him. Amara glared at Freja and said, "I told you to be quiet and not say anything!" With that she turned on her heels and stormed out of the tree house.

Fairies in general were no different than humans to look at. Most did not have any unusual features, which made blending in amongst humans so easy. They did not have wings, contrary to what people may think, but having said that, the magic they use is powerful enough to give them a temporary ability to fly, should they ever want to. This is most likely where the misconception comes from.

Fairies like humans, varied in height and weight, although it was extremely rare to ever see a fairy that was overweight. A fairy would typically be slender or muscular and light on their feet.

The life span of a fairy could be anything up to two hundred years, depending on their magic and how strong it is. Freja was sixty-eight years old, but she didn't look a day over twenty-one. Most fairies live a similar life span to a human, because they only ever practice magic on a small scale.

A Fairy thrives on the pain of others, whether it is human, elves, giant's and even animals. Some fairies prefer to act on a smaller scale, they opt to keep things simple, like - moving a chair from a human as they go to sit down, causing them to injure themselves.

Others like to cause trouble on a slightly bigger scale; like instigate an accident on a road, causing injury to multiple humans and leaving chaos in its wake.

These acts make up the large volume of fairies, past and present.

Then, there are the Kane's and a handful of others that wish to cause chaos on a much larger and devastating scale, resulting in mass death and grief. The ability to cause greater destruction is again dependent on the strength of the magic they behold.

The Kane family are the most powerful of all.

In the past, using magic - these fairies would influence other humans to carry out the vile acts, but as time has gone on, fairies like Kais Kane and his deluded followers have committed terrible acts of violence and terror themselves. Fairies that were once noted for their troublemaking schemes were now being feared as cold-blooded murderers. The worst fairies can manipulate a human mind to commit an act of violence that can kill thousands of humans. People call these 'terrorist attacks' but little do they know, it's simply a fairy using mind control to brainwash a human to kill for them.

They can get inside the heads of weak willed people, sometimes using the same human for multiple crimes. We know these people better as serial killers. The

Kane family had pulled off one of the world's most memorable mass murders in 2001. Kais Kane laughed as he used his magic to send an aeroplane into an iconic landmark, which resulted in sending two skyscraper buildings, crashing to the ground. The world stood still on this day as they mourned an attack which the fairies were never held accountable for.

In 1605 a man named Guy tried to blow up the Houses of Parliament, the mastermind behind this failed gunpowder plot was never known to the human world. The real architect was Abigor Kane, Kais Kane's grandfather. His plan failed on the 5th November, because an elf had intercepted the attack.

These are all games played by the fairies in a war between good and bad. You see, humans are not hostile beings by nature, it is not in their genetic make up to be evil. The evil comes from an external source. When a human being is created, they are so, with unconditional love of the world and everything in it. Many mythical creatures have died at the hands of fairies when they tried to stop them.

However, fairies have become extremely powerful, so much so, that the creatures of all realms have no choice but to unite in a bid to stop them.

CHAPTER NINE

Lauren had spent a week now learning how to cover her thoughts. She had been with Jared all day, every day for seven days. She was not complaining of course, in fact Jared was becoming an addiction for Lauren: she craved his presence.

Being around Jared made her feel like the best possible version of herself. He made her feel calm and protected. Lauren felt she was stronger by his side and had an even stronger sensation within her soul that her future would see him by her side. Now that she had learnt to cover her thoughts – she could go back to thinking like a normal person without her supernatural friends being able to hear them!

Jared, Jonty and Kymmie had been kind to Lauren. Much of what they heard her think, they kept to themselves, not wanting to embarrass her. Her mythical friends had come to really respect Lauren, partly because her vulnerability was exposed and they were able to see the real girl inside: see that she really was a kind and compassionate young woman. In addition to this, they also saw what humans never did and that was the hurt that she had carried inside for such a long time. The hurt of not knowing her father, never really knowing any of her family or where they came from. Lauren never really knew who she was and that was painful. Lauren had been strong, you would know that she held so much self-disapproval inside, she had never acted out or held anyone accountable for her shortfalls, she simply, pulled up her boot straps and got on with life.

Lauren was on the front porch steps of Jared's family home. She had knocked on the door and was now sitting in the sunshine waiting for him to come outside. They had arranged to take a picnic into the woods to celebrate the hard work Lauren had done in the past week and finally being able to shield her thoughts. Lauren was secretly hoping that this was a date. She heard the door open behind her and as she turned, she saw Jared standing in the doorway, his blue eyes glistening and at that moment, every single thought disappeared from her mind and all she could see was him.

A bomb could have gone off beside her and she wouldn't have known – she was falling, falling hard for him and she knew there was nothing she could do to stop it. To Lauren, Jared's eyes felt like home, some intense rich feeling deep within her very core, like they had known each other in lifetimes before.

Jared leaned down to help Lauren up. As their hands touched, they both felt a surge of energy run through their bodies. He smiled at Lauren, gently drawing her towards him as he pulled her up. They were standing inches apart, looking deeply into each other's eyes: both completely drowning in each other's spirits. Jared finally broke the silence, "Shall we go, Miss Fisher? – the Safe Haven is at least an hour's walk."

"What?"

Lauren gasped, "I can't go there Jared, you know what happened last time I went!"

As Lauren recalled, she fainted on her first ever meeting with Jared, she was embarrassed and had no desire for Jared to see her in that state again. Jared chuckled to himself.

"Lauren, you have strengthened so much since then, it's time for us to try again."

Lauren looked into his eyes and immediately agreed. Holding his gaze as she walked past him, Lauren whispered, "Those eyes are going to get me into a whole heap of trouble you know."

Jared and Lauren set off on their journey to the Safe Haven. They had barely reached the woods before Lauren began quizzing him about the history of this so called special place. She had so many questions, like, what sat beyond the walls and why could she feel that immense heat?

"The Safe Haven is a place that only elves can enter, it's like a refuge for us," Jared put his arm around Lauren's shoulders.

He went on to explain to Lauren that the reason she felt the heat was because this was the magical spell placed around the Haven to keep all creatures and humans out except elves. Jared and Jade were surprised that Lauren had the reaction that she did, being that she was a changeling. They assumed that the elf blood in her would be enough.

The trouble was, Lauren did not know her heritage and the supernatural part of her had never been triggered, Jared was hoping that this time, with all the practicing and being around her fellow elves, it would be enough to surpass the spell. Lauren just needed to believe in who she really was.

The pair talked for most of the walk, they had long moments of silence between them, although these moments were not awkward: they were perfect. Jared and Lauren had chemistry between them and during the silent moments, it was like their souls were communicating on a deep spiritual level. This kind of intensity towards another person was completely new to him and to her, they both were completely petrified of their feelings yet at the same time, they both knew that this was categorically right. Jared finally did what Lauren had been hoping for all day, he took her hand. Ever since they had left the farm, Lauren had been desperate for Jared to entwine his fingers with hers, just like all lead males did in all her favourite movies. She was too afraid to make the first move but now he had and it was exactly how she'd imagined it.

Fireworks were going off in her mind, her fingertips tingled. She was happy. Nothing mattered in that moment, it was utter bliss. They held hands the rest of the way, casually catching each other's eyes as they walked side by side.

As the pair approached the Safe Haven, Lauren began to worry. What if she was not worthy enough to enter? What if history were to repeat itself and she was to pass out in front of Jared all over again?

As these thoughts ran frantically through her mind, Lauren could feel warmth begin to set into her body.

"Oh no,"

Lauren said aloud, "it is happening."

Lauren started to feel disappointed, was she not good enough? The heat was coming on stronger and stronger.

Then suddenly an intense and prominent thought flooded to the forefront of all the chaos and chatter filling up in her brain. A vibrant voice like a wave of certainty echoed throughout and pushed all the fear fuelled thoughts aside. *'Lauren, you are strong and pure – stare alta et recta.'*

Lauren had studied basic Latin in school, so knew that the voice was telling her to stand straight and tall. This encouraging male, although she did not know who the voice belonged to was enough to make Lauren feel confident and strong. She stood up straight, shoulders back and a took a few deep breaths. She was ready, she was going through that gap in the rocks and nothing was going to stop her, "I am an elf!" She stated aloud.

And with that, she marched right up to the gap between the two rocks. No heat, no high-pitched frequency ringing through her ears. She simply waltzed up to the haven and straight through the entrance just like she would step through her own bedroom door.

Jared stood amazed, after a few seconds, he realised he was gawping and quickly hurried after her. Lauren looked around, she had no idea what to expect but she was impressed.

A sea of bright coloured flowers and fresh green leaves covered the ground. Cerise pinks, yellows, blues and purples were amongst a few of the vibrant colours. It was perfect, every single flower had bloomed flawlessly.

There was a narrow stone path winding itself through the sea of multicoloured petals. Lauren could smell the sweet aroma, she felt safe here. They both began to walk down the uneven path.

Lauren felt the summer breeze sweep across her face, the sun flickering through the leaves as the wind moved them to and fro.

As they walked further into the haven, the trees started to close in closer to the path.

They were now walking on along a dirt track path, through a wooded area. The trees stood like soldiers all around them, their thin trunks, wonderfully aligned. When designing, The Safe Haven, every single aspect of this place had been strategically and thoughtfully planned.

Not a leave nor stone was out of place.

Further along the walkway, a few old rough stones formed steps which lead down to an open meadow.

A huge willow tree sat majestically in the middle of the open field. Lauren could tell this tree had been there for many years. She could feel the spiritual intensity all around her. This place was special, Lauren just knew. On the opposite side of the meadow was a huge stately home. The property was grand, it had twenty-eight windows, just on the front facing side of the building. It was built using classic rocks in a puzzle of stones and cement, with charcoal grey slats for the roof. The front garden had green bushes sculpted into various shapes. There was a gravel path leading up to the front door and in the centre of the garden, there was a grand, marble water fountain.

Lauren could see behind the house sat a huge clear water lake. A small white rowing boat was moored up to the wooden pier. The water was turquoise and completely still.

The pair walked around the willow tree and took a seat on a wooden bench on the other side, just in front of the house. Jared explained the heritage of the tree, he told Lauren that one of the very first elves to have ever walked this earth was called Nevaeh.

She was gracious, kind and very beautiful. Nevaeh lovingly protected all creatures and encouraged growth and balance of all earthly living beings. She created all goodness on earth. Although, Nevaeh was not alone in her creating. As with anything, there is always an opposite. Nevaeh was the creator of love and light and her sister, Demelza, was the creator of darkness and ego. Their souls were formed from the same flame, they separated and became the complete opposites.

Nevaeh had ebony skin, rich purple eyes and long golden hair. Demelza on the other hand, had ivory skin, jet black hair which was cropped short around her chiselled jawline and her eyes were the darkest shade of brown.

Even though they wanted to create a different earth from one another, they were connected and had always lived side by side. They loved and respected each other, neither would have ever done anything to hurt the other. The strongest of sisterly bonds. That was until one day, they both fell in love with the same man.

"Typical,"

Lauren rolled her eyes.

"I knew a man would have something to do with it!"

Jared smiled and continued, the twin flames both fell in love with a human man called Solomon Godwin, an explorer.

Solomon was a tall, rugged man. He had long brown hair and a wild beard. He was a plain looking man but had the most beautiful and caring heart. He loved to seek adventure, travelling the earth in search for new cultures and lands. He met the sisters separately on his travels and began a love affair with both.

The sisters were so different, the purest of each side of the ying and yang. Nevaeh offering him pure unconditional love and support. Demelza, gave him fierce adventure and wild passion. He fell for both women, as they each offered something different, something the other could not and he of course could not resist.

The day eventually came where Solomon had to choose which of them he wanted to spend the rest of his mortal days with and he chose Nevaeh. Demelza was heartbroken, she had loved a mere human man and had devoted her love to him, only to find, he loved her sister more than her. The pain and shame of it was all too much for Demelza, she was so furious upon learning the betrayal that she ripped his heart from his chest in act of pure bitter spite.

The relationship between the two sisters turned into a war of good and evil. The rejection Demelza felt sent the already dark soul into blackness. She began on the path of earthly destruction and no one could stop her.

Over time she became more powerful than Nevaeh. She had a lot of followers who supported her crusade. Even turning humans into soldiers by giving them magical powers, we know them better as witches who use black magic.

Nevaeh tried desperately to stop her sister without hurting her, she was so upset about the death of Solomon, but she was even more sad that his choice had broken her beautiful sister this way. Nevaeh believed that her sibling would never truly hurt her, but her naïve love resulted in Demelza killing Nevaeh.

She died in this very spot, her body sunk into the ground and this willow tree grew. It has been protecting this area ever since. Elves come here to gain strength and healing when dealing with the evil in the world. The house behind is used mostly for training young elves that show warrior strength. It is where they come to learn how to use their powers for good and to protect the human race.

Lauren was speechless, she stared intensely at the old willow tree. Sadness filled her heart.

Finally, Lauren asked Jared, "What happened to Demelza?"

"Well."

Jared began, "A war broke out and all of Nevaeh's creations fought hard to protect the earth and good things. The resistance was led by Alfonso Valentin, an ancestor of yours, Lauren. They imprisoned Demelza in another world. You probably know this place as purgatory. Your family have been protectors of humans and this world for thousands of years. The Valentin family is the most powerful and respected of all."

Lauren now had tears rolling down her cheeks. After all these years, she was getting the answers she had always wanted. Her heritage was so much more than she could have ever imagined. She belonged to something bigger than the life she had led in Middle Keynes.

Lauren and Jared stayed at the Safe Haven for a few hours, they didn't enter the house, even though Lauren was desperate to see the inside. Jared had told her that they needed permission from a high-ranking elf before they could go inside. They wandered the grounds and Jared told Lauren of many historical tales involving her blood line. Lauren was proud and quickly falling in love with Jared. The way he moved, his voice, the way he gazed into Lauren's eyes. Yes, there was no denying it, she was head over heels in love and completely screwed!

CHAPTER TEN

Amara and Freja were sat by the lake. The night sky was lit by a full moon and thousands of stars floating above, against the back drop of the sunless sky. They were sitting in silence, gazing across the still water. Freya was agitated.

"What is wrong with you tonight Freja?" Amara was aware that Freja had something on her mind: she was fidgeting and huffing like a disgruntled teenager, holding a small branch in her hands, almost as though she was about to use it as a weapon.

"Gregory was supposed to be here ten minutes ago, that is what is wrong with me."

Freja's voice was now sharp and stern.

Amara was confused.

"And Gregory is?"

"Gregory is a kappa,"

Freja snapped, her voice becoming higher and more aggressive with each word, "who was meant to be here ten minutes ago!" With that Freja was on her feet and had snapped the branch she was holding in half. Freja had a bad temper. When she wanted something, she was desirable and she had perfected the art of nice. This was all an act though and as soon as she didn't get her way, her evil and bitter streak would pour out and she would bring hell to her mercy.

"Please do not tell me you have seduced a kappa? Freja, they are forbidden to make contact with us, you will get him killed!" Amara was concerned, not only for Gregory, but also for herself. She wanted off this stupid island and didn't want her idiotic sister to make things any worse.

"Mar, I am not bothered if he dies, as long as I get what I want, I don't care!"

Freja was now throwing the pieces of broken branch into the water, she was making threats about how as soon as she could, she would kill every single kappa in the lake, by ripping off their heads. Freja was furious, her eyes were glowing red and she was ready to kill, when all of a sudden there was movement in the water.

A young man emerged from the lake. He was very slim and very young; he looked about 17 years old. The hair on his head was a mousy brown, he hadn't yet grown any facial or body hair.

"Oh Gregory, you made it my love, I have been so very worried about you."

Amara rolled her eyes.

And with that, Freja had flipped the switch and on came her charming damsel routine.

Freja grabbed Gregory by the hand and led him off into the forest. Amara sat in disgust.

"What the heck does she want with that young kappa?"

Benny had joined Amara by the lake. Amara sighed and shook her head, "I have no idea, but no doubt we will all pay the price if it goes wrong."

Amara was the smarter of the two sisters, she was the tactful and intelligent planner and Freja was the aggressive foot soldier. Kais knew the strengths he had in each daughter and used those to his advantage.

"Hey Mar, can I ask you something?"

Benny was sweet and kind at heart. He was troublesome, that was obvious and he had done some of the most violent and brutal killings that Amara had ever seen by someone not Kais or Freja.

But even with this being said, deep down, he had a really caring nature and it was plain to see that he was guilty and remorseful of his actions, a trait with fairies do not possess, at all.

Sometimes Amara wondered if he really was a full blood fairy or whether he just put on an act to impress Kais. The fact that no one knew how or where he come from, just fuelled Amaras suspicion.

"What's up Benny?" Amara knew that Benny would never ask anything in front of Kais or Freja that would make him look weak. He trusted Amara. Although Benny was not particularly close to either of the sisters, he was far fonder of Amara.

"When we get off this island, what will you do? I mean, will you stay with us or will you go and find a new life alone?"

Amara stayed silent, she had thought about this a lot over the past eighteen years. If she did ever become free from this prison she wanted nothing more than to separate herself from her family. Of course, she would never admit that too them, especially not their father. Kais had always told his daughters that betrayal was punishable by death, and that if either of them ever want to go against him, they would no longer be part of the family and thus, he would kill them.

Kais did not give empty threats, he killed his own sister, Maya because she betrayed him years ago. He never told his daughters what it was she did to break his trust but whatever it was, it was enough for him to take a clip blade to her throat and end her life. Maya's name had never been mentioned since that brutal day, but knowing what her father had done to her aunt stayed with Amara.

Kais had told his daughters that Maya had begged for her life before she died, he wanted his own children to fear him and know he had no mercy.

So how could she leave? He would kill her too. Maya was in hiding for five years before she was killed. Kais had dedicated those five years to hunting her down and making her pay for what he called, the worse sin.

Amara turned to Benny and smiled. "We will all do as father says."

Meanwhile, Freja had led Gregory into a cave in the forest. She had already prepared the cave prior to Gregory arriving. There were candles all around the cave, petals from flowers covered the floor, giving the usually dark cold space a warm and romantic feel. Freja had laid a rug down on the floor and placed two cups of squeezed berry juice and some fresh fruit on the floor next to the rug. Freja sat down on the blanket, gazing up into Gregory's eyes. She was seducing the young, innocent boy. Freja was an expert in the art of seduction, she soon held out her hand and summoned him over.

Gregory swallowed hard and moved over to her, taking a seat beside flirtatious fairy. Gregory had clearly never been intimate with a woman before: he was shaking with nerves and had begun sweating. Freja gently whispered, "I think I am in love with you," into Gregory's ear. She started kissing his neck. Freja did not love the boy at all, in fact she didn't even like him but she wanted something from him and she knew sex was the easiest way for her to get it but unlike with most men, Freja had to fake an emotional connection first to get him into bed. The pair made love on the rug of the secluded cave. Freja had taken the boys virginity without any care at all.

Freja had spent the past six weeks getting close to Gregory, she had spotted him swimming close to the island and began removing her clothes in a sexual display to draw his attention. It worked and he had soon fallen for her charm.

Freja lay in his arms, her face cold and hard. Gregory on the other hand was beaming with joy. He began to tell Freja how he loved her and would do anything for her. Freja smiled, her plan had worked.

"Well, Gregory my sweet love, there is one teeny tiny thing you could do for me."

So, here it was, Freja was about to send Gregory off to gather some information for her. She was obsessed with Lauren's arrival, she wanted to know more: who she was and what had brought her to Eden. She asked Gregory to find out as much as he could about Lauren and report back to her. She told him that every time he did so, she would reward him with her love.

Of course, Gregory was young and foolish and believed wholeheartedly in her lies. She was his first love and he was completely blinded by it.

Gregory told Freja that there was a new girl in town and promised Freja he would return as soon as he could with the information she wanted. Gregory entered back into the water, felling like the luckiest boy in the world. Freja on the other hand, felt nothing. She walked over to the stream to wash the ruminants of Gregory from her skin. Freja had loved once before. It was a long time ago and she had never let herself get close to anybody since then. He was a fairy too, so powerful and bitter that Kais had welcomed him into the family as a son.

His name was Makkalai Radha, he had olive skin, black wavy hair and green eyes. He loved Freja, but he loved being part of the Kane family more. The power and respect he had, just from being with her meant, he would never leave her, never by choice anyway.

He was killed in the great battle in Sumatra. Back in 2004, there was a huge war that broke out between the fairies and the kappa in the Indian Ocean. The fairies had wanted to wipe out the kappa, so in the late evening of Christmas day, they formed an army to take to the seas, no one had predicted this devastation happening, which resulted in 250,000 human fatalities, not to mention thousands of fairies and kappa and millions of marine creatures.

Freja was beyond devastated and as she sat by the stream, she felt empty and ashamed. She had let Gregory touch her, even after what his kind did to her one true love.

Makkalai's death was not quick, he had suffered and Freja was helpless to save him. This had been one of the reasons Freja had struggled to come to terms with her loss. She blamed herself every day for not being able to do more for him. One tear rolled down her cheek as she held onto the necklace around her neck, that Makkalai had given her. She vowed to kill every, last one of them as soon as she had the information that she needed, starting with Gregory. The humans believed the Tsunami that day was a natural disaster, they had even made a film about the tragedy and not a single mythical creature was mentioned.

Kais had also taken Makkalai's death very badly. He had always wanted two sons, not daughters. Benny and Makkalai were his prodigy's and losing Makkalai was like losing his eldest son.

He holds a very long and venomous grudge against the elder of the kappa, Kais has vowed that he will have his revenge and it will be served on an ice platter.

Benny resented the relationship between Makkalai and Kais, he always felt that Kais favoured Makkalai over him and nothing he would do, would ever be as good as Makkalai had done, even though Benny was the stronger and more compelling of the two.

Benny and Makkalai had never really seen eye to eye and had never bonded as brothers. His death had no effect on Benny, if anything, he was pleased to have rid of him. Although he thought this, he would never dare speak ill of Makkalai to Kais or Freja. They would more than likely kill him on the spot just for thinking it.

The next morning, Freja awoke to find Gregory standing over her as she lay in her bed. He had startled her and reaction had him flying across the room and smashing onto the wooden slat wall. Freja could move a bus with the wave of her hand, so Gregory, was like swatting a fly. Gregory scrambled to get up, he had his hands out in front of him, shouting, "it's me, its Gregory."

Freja rolled her eyes, "What are you doing here Gregory?"

Gregory's voice was shaking as he told her, he had the information she wanted. Freja quickly changed her tone, "Oh, my sweet love, you cannot just walk in a women's bedroom and frighten her, sit down and tell me what you know."

Gregory sheepishly walked over to the bed and sat down next to Freja, he told her that Lauren was the daughter of Zenon Valentin and that when she arrived into town, she had no idea who she really was. Freja stayed silent whilst Gregory spoke.

"The best part is, she is here and unprotected by the elders!"

He laughed aloud. Freja smiled, "Thank you, my love, you have been very helpful."

Gregory soon left, he had to sneak back into the water without being noticed by any other kappa. The kappa were forbidden to ever contact the fairies; they were to guard the island only, to ensure nothing or no one got on or off the island. The kappa knew how dangerous the fairies were. Gregory was not born when Freja and the other fairies were imprisoned and although he had heard the stories, he did not fully understand how bad things were.

He was easy to manipulate. In his mind, Gregory did not see what all the fuss was. Freja had brain washed him into believing that she was the victim of a terrible misunderstanding.

Of course, she neglected to tell him the part where she had single-handedly killed sixteen kappa when they tried to imprison her and not to mention a few thousand in the Sumatra battle. Freja was ruthless and it was only time before Gregory would see this.

Freja rushed off to tell Kais her findings. She knew such information would please him and she wanted nothing more than to please her father. Kais was in his tree house standing by the window on the far side, overlooking the lake. He was a tall, stocky man with thin blonde hair and small oval shaped eyes, black and empty. Just like his soul. His complexion was pale and his aura was cold and frightening. To look at this man, you would never believe that the two beautiful fairies were his daughters. He was not an attractive man at all and he had no charm or character either. Some say his wife Soriah was only attracted to his power, which is believable as other than his strength, he has nothing else going for him. Freja and Amara's mother, was killed just prior to their imprisonment. She had been the reason Nicole and Jens parents had died. Using magic, she locked the car doors with them inside and set the car on fire. They burned alive as Soriah stood by, watching and laughing. She had started to lose her mind; her actions were unstable and she had started to make silly mistakes. She was desperate for Kais to make a move against the elves and so, she provoked the other side, which lead to her death.

Soriah, like her daughters, was exceptionally good looking. Her hair was long, curly and jet black. She had silver eyes and an olive complexion. Soriah was cruel and vindictive and didn't have a single maternal bone in her petit, toned body.

Kais and Soriah made the perfect couple, or the worst. Two people who loved death and sadness so much, it made them very powerful.

Soriah had a strong accent from overseas, she often spoke in the tongue of the devil - Kaliska, a language used during spell casting to communicate with Demelza. When Soriah was alive, she had an army of human witches at her beck and call. They saw her as their goddess, their queen of darkness. Soriah was a lot older than Kais, he was now the most powerful Fairy in the world, and is a staggering 652 years old, but Soriah was born 231 years before him and during her lifetime, she was the most feared of them all, not because she had power, but because she was smart and creative. She had managed to create loop holes that no other mystical creature ever had.

In 1556, Soriah tried to raise the dead. She had spent years perfecting a spell and honing her abilities, for this moment. In the Wei River Valley in Shaanxi Province, 461 years ago, Soriah attempted to raise the dead souls of her loyal army, whom had died in her name.

The sacrifice would have been her life for theirs. Kais had found out that she was offering her soul in exchange for those whom had worshipped her and interrupted the ritual. The event had been catastrophic, causing an earthquake that killed over 830,000 human lives. Again, the mortals of the world had never known what had really happened on that January morning.

Kais and his daughters wanted retribution for her death, the only thing standing in their way, was their imprisonment on Fey Forest.

As Freja entered she saw her father speaking, what sounded like Kaliska, into a small object. When he noticed her entrance, he quickly put it in his pocket.

"Father, I have some information for you, the girl I told you about, she is…"

Kais put his hand out to hush her.

"She is the daughter of Zenon Valentin," he smiled, "I wondered how long it would take you to find it out, you are your mother's daughter alright."

Freja smiled. Her father praised her and that made her feel proud.

She asked him how he knew. There was silence, as Kais stood with his back to Freja. Kais had never had much trust in either of his daughters. Freja had always been desperate to be his right hand and after Makkalai's death, she hoped he would finally promote her to be his adviser, but he never did. In fact, Kais had been keeping many secrets from his daughters and Benny over the years, too many for most to keep track of, but Kais was calculated in his lies and he had managed to hide them well, but it was now time for him to share one of his secrets, whether he wanted it or not. He would need them all to be ready for what was coming.

Kais finally turned around and explained to Freja, that he had been in communication with some of her late mother's witches. They too were looking to avenge her death and so had managed to find a way to get a communication device to him. With that he pulled out the small object from his pocket. At first glance, the object looked like a rusty golden, compact mirror, but when it opened, Freja could see, day glo green and pearlescent white lights shining out in a perpetual motion. The vibrant colours were mesmerizing as they flowed and danced around the base of the timeworn object, just like the Northern Lights across the Scandinavian skies. Kais, explained that the modern-day witches had found a way to communicate with him through the Aurora Borealis over Norway. The lights were a magic made port, to connect realms within the universe.

Kais had known about Lauren being in Eden as he was the one who orchestrated her moving here in the first place, by faking a trip for her mother, forcing her to send Lauren to the only family she had. He told Freja how he had planned to bring Lauren here, with the intention of using her life as a trade for their freedom.

"Freya, the reason you can feel her is because before your mother died, she used her final breath to cast a linking spell between you and her. I have been able to tap into this connection. Everything you have been seeing around her all these years, has led me to finding her location."

Freja was shocked, she had so many questions, like, if he could find her all along, why had it taken him 18 years!

"The elves had placed a cloaking spell around her. I have had witches searching high and low for her and as soon as they found her, I brought her here."

Freja was upset that he hadn't included her in his plans sooner, perhaps she could have helped him more. She worried that he did not trust her enough to assist him. Kais told Freja that he was pleased with her using her initiative to find out information from the kappa, then asked her to leave and go back to her tree house. Feeling rejected, Freja left Kais and retreated to her tree.

CHAPTER ELEVEN

It was Jonty's Birthday and Kymmie had organised a picnic party in the woods. Jared, Lauren and Jade had all gathered to help him celebrate. Word had now somehow travelled about Lauren's arrival and other mystical beings had learned of her heritage. Jared's parents had still not returned to town and the group had been worrying about what was going on. Many elders were have said to have disappeared, and it was thought they had gone off to a secret location for an emergency meeting.

It was rare for all the elders to gather together, this only happened in cases of an emergency. This had concerned Lauren deeply, so the party was a way for the group to relax and have some fun. Lauren wanted Jonty and the others to have a 'normal' teenage day for a change, without having to worry about what was going on.

Lauren had no idea why her arrival was such a big deal, she didn't ask to be here, she was sent by her mother, whom she hadn't heard from since being here. Aunt Jen didn't seem concerned, she said that Nicole probably didn't have access to a phone on her trip and said not to worry. Aunt Jen had assured Lauren that as they had won a competition for a trip around the world, the trip organiser would surely contact her if there was a problem.

It was unusual for Nicole not to send Lauren pictures of her adventures and although Nicole was bit eccentric and loose, she had always made sure that when Lauren went away on school trips or camping weekends with friends, that Lauren would call or text her daily to let her know she was safe and when Nicole went to meet Dale, she had video called Lauren three times, a day, just to check that Lauren was ok without her mother there.

It seemed odd to Lauren that Nicole would just stop all contact completely, but she thought Jen was probably right, why would anyone want to keep checking in back home, when you are having the time of your life!

A thought came to Lauren... What if the trip was a hoax, intended to bring Lauren to Eden and her mum and Dale had really been kidnapped? Lauren remembered her mother saying she didn't recall entering any competition, so it was a bit strange that they did win. Lauren chuckled to herself, "this place is starting make me paranoid,"

she muttered as she laid a big red blanket on the ground. Jade and Lauren had become very close in the time that she had been in Eden. Jade was the most beautiful and kind person Lauren had ever met. Back in Middle Keynes, pretty girls were always really mean, it was almost as though teenage girls were not able to have both traits; you were either a pretty bitch or a sweet plain Jane.

But Jade was different, she was pure and gracious. Jade caught Lauren's eye and she began to walk towards Lauren. Her walk was more like an angelic float. Her long auburn hair was gently blowing in the breeze and her jade green eyes sparkled in the sunlight. She smiled sweetly at Lauren.

"You look lovely today Lauren."

Lauren looked down at her old, slightly discoloured, flower-patterned dress and then looked at Jades elegant, olive, chiffon dress.

"It should be illegal to look as good as you Jade," Lauren followed this this statement with a smile and a wink.

Jade took Lauren's hand and said again, you really do look lovely."

Lauren laughed and rolled her eyes, "why do you have to be so damn nice all the time."

The picnic party was underway and the group were laughing and dancing along to music playing on Lauren's phone. Jared and Jade had made a variety of sandwiches, Lauren and Jen had baked a big chocolate fudge cake and Kymmie and Jonty provided the group with the refreshments. They had left their troubles behind them and were having fun. The hours rushed by them and they continued their party late into the evening. It must have been around 10pm when they decided to get a fire going. They were telling each other funny stories about their lives as they sat around the orange flames. It was special and would have been a perfect end to their evening. But the night was not over and it was not destined to end on such a happy high. In fact, what was in store was much different.

~

Back on Fey Forest, Freja had stormed off into the trees. She was furious with her father for keeping secrets from her. She kept wondering, what did she need to do to make him respect her? When Freja had met Makkalai, Kais had all but discarded Freja. Amara was living her own life, far away from the rest of the Kane family and her mother, Soriah, had been completely consumed with her lackey witches. So, when Makkalai showed some interest in her, it made her feel valuable and wanted. She had, up to then, felt worthless and unimportant to anyone, including her own family. Makkalai and Freja, being together had made Kais notice her. Suddenly, she was involved in discussions.

She was never allowed to talk, but she was happy to just be invited to listen in. Makkalai adored Freja and so, encouraged Kais to keep her in their inner circle. Kais never shunned Freja after Makkalai's murder, but he also never brought her any closer and she then found herself feeling not only, alone and broken hearted but also non-essential in her father's life.

Freja had now reached the north side of the island. She sat by the water's edge and thought about her beloved, Makkalai. 'There must be a way to bring him back?'

She thought to herself. Soriah had designed a spell to raise the dead years ago, and it would have worked had Kais not intervened. The sacrifice for many lives was her own soul, but Freja knew that the offering for one soul to be brought back to the earthly plain, would not be so great.

Freja ran back as fast as she could. When she reached her sister's tree house, she ascended upwards into the air and landed onto the roof. Freja was weightless, she jumped with ease and poise and made hardly any noise when her feet touched the wooden surface below her. She then climbed down through Amaras window. Amara was sat on the floor, crossed legged in the lotus position. Meditation was a common part of the fairy's day. Clearing their conscious minds, enabled them to draw more power from the energy around them. Kais would sometimes sit for days in a trance and seeing as the girls and Benny had nothing else to do with their days, they too made meditation a part of their daily routine. Freja rushed over to Amara and kneeled down beside her. Amara could feel her sisters stare and soon opened one eye.

"What do you want." She snapped.

"Mar, I need your help,"

Freja put her hand on her sister's arm as she whispered, "I need you to help me steal something from our father."

Amara jumped up and shouted, "You must be joking Freja, he will kill us both!"

Freja, quickly got up to and tried to hush her sister, "Shhh, Mar listen, he has mother's grimoire and I just need one little spell from it."

Amara was flustered, this was a big ask from Freja. Kais would be furious if he found out they had been snooping in his tree house, let alone stealing one of his late wife's spells!

"What spell, could you possibly need so badly, that you would risk both of our lives for it." Amara was now speaking quietly but her words were as sharp as a knife.

Freja put both of her hands on her hips and took a deep breath in, "I want to bring Makkalai back."

Freja nodded her head in self approval, she wanted her love back and she wanted her father's attention. This was the only way to get what she wanted.

Amara stood in silence, her jaw was dropped and she had a blank and confused expression. After a few moments of getting her head around her sister's words, she finally spoke, "You are insane! Even if we did manage to get the spell, without being caught, we don't have any of the enchanted herbs or compounds that you would need to cast it, here on this poxy island."

Freja was excited, "yes, but Mar, we won't be here for much longer, father has a plan to get us off the island, we are going to be free before the week is up!"

~

It was Kymmie's turn to tell a funny story of her childhood and everyone was laughing. She was just about to tell the punchline when all of a sudden, she froze, fear set into her face.

"Kymmie, are you alright?" said Jared.

The group of friends grew concerned. Kymmie was as still as a rock. She finally mumbled…

"Something is here."

Nymphs were created to help the land to flourish and grow, but they were also known for their psychic abilities; they could feel when danger was around. They had always been strong alliances to elves during battles as they were able to predetermine whether a battle plan would work in their favour or not, needless to say, the group was now becoming extremely worried by Kymmie's petrified state.

Kymmie stood on her feet, looking frantically around her. The others had now joined her and were glancing around to try and see if there was any danger, but the woods were in complete darkness and through the trees, all they could see was blackness.

"Anrme ulwa senrti wai.

Anrme ulwa senrti wai. Anrme ulwa senrti wai."

Out of nowhere, figures emerged from the trees and surrounded the young friends. The mystery intruders were dressed in floor length, rich purple velvet cloaks. Their hoods were up, covering their faces. The robes had golden inscriptions sewn onto the arms, Lauren did not know what they meant, but had a feeling the words were from the language they spoke which she did not recognise. They were chanting these words, over and over. The words were a spell spoken in Kaliska. The chant brought all of them to their knees, apart from Lauren. She was shaking and looking around at her friends, whom all seemed to be in agonising pain on the floor around her.

"What is happening!"

Lauren ran over to Jared to try and help him. Jared was unresponsive, his eyes had rolled into the back of his head. Lauren looked around at the others and noticed that they too, were in the same state as Jared.

"What have you done to them!"

Lauren stood up and shouted to hostile figures, who had now formed a tight circle around her and her friends.

"Stop it, stop it!"

Lauren was screaming and crying.

One of the figures moved forward and broke formation from the circle, the rest continued to chant...

"Anrme ulwa senrti wai."

The stranger pulled back her hood. It was a young blonde-haired woman. She looked not much older than Lauren, in fact, she looked like a normal teenage girl. Lauren was confused, "Why are you doing this?"

The girl smiled and purred, "Hello Lauren, I am Abigail. Come with me now and no one will get hurt."

These were people, normal human beings who had dedicated their life to Witchcraft, Black Magic and Demelza. They had chosen the life of evil over good.

"Why are you doing this?"

Lauren was still shaking and fighting back tears.

"Come with us now of your own free will or I will kill your friends."

Abigail spoke with no emotion. She was cold, but Lauren did not believe her threats. She refused to go with Abigail and demanded she stop hurting her friends at once. Lauren thought nothing of her words, Abigail wasn't a threat, she was a kid, Lauren would never in her wildest nightmares, ever of been able to predict what happened next.

Abigail walked slowly over to Jonty, she kept her eyes locked onto Laurens, she never even blinked, she just stared intensely.

Lauren felt chills down her spine. When Abigail got next to the gentle, half giant, she knelt down beside him. Stroking his head as she continued to look Lauren dead straight in the eyes. Abigail then pulled a sharp blade from the cloak pocket and grabbed Jonty by the hair, before Lauren could even scream no, Abigail had taken the knife to his throat and with one clean movement the wicked deed was done.

Lauren screamed and ran over to Jonty. She was crying for him to wake up whilst trying to stop the bleeding by covering the wound with her hands. Abigail stood over them and repeated to Lauren, "Come with us now, or I will kill all of your friends."

Lauren sobbed uncontrollably.

"Wake up, please Jonty, wake up."

The blood was gushing from his neck. Lauren took her white cardigan off and used it to apply pressure to his wound. Within seconds the once crisp white garment had been completely blood soaked. She looked around at her friends laying helplessly on the floor, they were unaware that Jonty was choking on his own blood, unaware that they too would face this fate if Lauren did not leave with them.

Lauren looked down at Jonty and saw he had stopped breathing.

Abigail had killed him in cold blood. Realising that Abigail was serious and not wanting the others to die too, Lauren got up still sobbing and went with the hooded witches. She turned back to see her friends lying unconscious on the ground and Jonty's lifeless body just left in a pool of his own blood. Lauren whispered, "I'm so sorry" as they disappeared through the trees into darkness.

By the time Jared and the others came around, Lauren and the witches were long gone. The group looked around them as they got up from the ground, they were trying to remember what had happened. Kymmie was the first one to see Jonty, she screamed when she saw her best friend lying dead, covered in blood.

Jared desperately shouted for Lauren, "where is she, LAUREN!"

Jared loved her unconditionally and the thought of her being hurt was too much for him, he ran into the woods to search for her but the trail was cold and he soon returned to the others. Jade was trying desperately to resuscitate Jonty, but it was too late. He had bled to death and the group of friends had no idea what had happened to him or what had happened to Lauren.

For all they knew, she too could be laying in a ditch somewhere with her throat slashed. The trio sat in silence around Jonty's lifeless body, tears pouring. Jonty was a gentle giant and did not deserve such a cruel and untimely death.

CHAPTER TWELVE

Lauren had been tied up and left in the back of a van for more than two hours. She had no idea where these people were taking her or why. She looked down at her blood covered body and wept. She was full of guilt and sorrow. If only she had done what they'd asked, if only she had listened. Jonty would still be alive. Lauren believed that Jonty's death was her fault: that she killed him. She felt as though the others would think this too. Lauren blamed herself, so whatever would happen to her next, she didn't care. She deserved any pain and punishment she got.

Lauren had no idea that Kais had already told Abigail to kill Jonty. This was not her fault, Abigail would have killed him regardless, but Lauren did not know this. Kais had wanted to send a clear message to the elders, he wanted to kill an innocent changeling like Lauren and being that Jonty was the only other changeling and his parents were both dead, he was a good choice. Plus, Kais hated giants, he thought of them as the plague, so Jonty was just a purification kill to him.

The van was dark and cold, Lauren was shivering. She was still putting herself through emotional turmoil when the vehicle came to a halt. The back doors swung open and a hooded witch learned in and grabbed her by her wrists.

"Where are we?"

Lauren demanded. The witch ignored her and pulled her aggressively from the van. Lauren lost her footing and fell into the muddy ground. She tried to look around to see where she was but it was still dark. As she turned around, Lauren saw that she was outside a huge elegant house, in the countryside. The house clearly belonged to someone very wealthy. There were acres and acres of land around them, she had been brought to a secluded property in the middle of nowhere. The hooded witch pulled Lauren to her feet and forced her to walk towards the big house. Lauren could see Abigail standing on the porch, waiting.

As Lauren entered the stately home, she noticed how sophisticated the rooms were decorated. Not what she was expecting at all.

"Take her to the basement,"

Abigail shouted to the person still holding onto Laurens wrists. As they pushed Lauren down the corridor, Lauren looked at the walls and saw family portraits framed upon the wall along the hallway. Abigail's family pictures. There was a photograph of Abigail and her parents on vacation, one of Abigail graduating and her parents wedding picture. This was Abigail's family home; she was a normal teenager with wealthy parents, why was she doing this? As Lauren was dragged closer to the basement she began to scream for help. Surely Abigail's parents where around, they wouldn't allow this to happen.

"Help, help me!"

The hooded figure laughed at Lauren's pleas for help.

"No one can hear you."

And with that, the witch pushed Lauren down the steps of the basement. The fall knocked Lauren unconscious and the basement door slammed shut, leaving Lauren on the floor and once again, alone in darkness.

Abigail was standing in her kitchen. She was holding a communication device similar to the one Kais was holding when Freja interrupted him in his tree house, back in Fey Forest.

She opened the device and said a few words in Kaliska,

"Opli kamaw suri."

The words were a chant which connected the device to Kais. As she said them, the device began to glow and the green and white lights, shone out of the device.

"We have the girl, just like you asked my

Lord."

Abigail was communicating with someone.

"What would you like us to do?"

There was a moment's silence, "Yes my Lord, as you wish."

And with that, Abigail closed the device.

When Lauren came to, she could hear the witches talking upstairs. She heard one concerned voice ask,

"Well how long do we have to wait Abigail?

Your parents are only away for the weekend!

If they come home and catch us, we will all be in trouble!"

"Quiet, you fool!"

Lauren recognised Abigail's voice, "We keep her here until he tells us otherwise!"

He? Lauren wondered who 'he' was. Clearly Abigail and her friends were taking orders from somebody. These were just college kids, practicing black magic without their parents' knowledge. They had joined some cult, which had turned them into kidnappers and by the sounds of it, some of them were starting to regret their involvement.

Abigail's voice got louder.

"We pledged our allegiance to Kais Kane, so if any of you have a problem, I am sure he would love to hear about it!"

There was silence. Lauren understood now, they were working for the fairies, the worst Fairy in fact. They were working for Kais. He had recruited a group of witches, long before the imprisonment. After eighteen years, the coven's powers had diminished and the younger generation where required to step up and take over. Abigail had always been a promising young witch, so the coven had chosen her to lead.

Kais had tasked her with the job of forming a new and stronger army. Witches were far and few between these days, most were inexperienced, wishful thinkers. She had rallied up a bunch of novice witches to help carry out the mission. As a group, they were very powerful. The way they took all the others to the floor with just a few words back in the woods, just showed how as a coven, they were strong. Lauren thought that maybe if she could break the circle within the coven - they clearly already had weak links, then maybe she could find a way to escape. But where would she go? She couldn't return to Eden. They would hate her when they found out that she was the reason their beloved Jonty was killed. She couldn't go to her mother as she had no idea where in the world she was.

No, Lauren maintained her belief, she just had to face her punishment. She had failed her friends and now she would endure the consequences.

~

Back in Eden, word had spread about Lauren's abduction and the death of Jonty. The humans were oblivious that anything had happened but the mystic beings were becoming frightened and apprehensive. Eden hadn't experienced any suspicious deaths since the fairies were banished to Fey Forest eighteen years ago so, naturally panic was setting in all around. The elders had still not returned and there had been no word from them, which just fuelled the uneasiness even more. Jared, Jade and Kymmie decided between them, that they would take it upon themselves to find Lauren and save her. After all, they couldn't just leave her, she was their friend and they had lost too much already.

Aunt Jen had been working days and nights at different ranches, miles outside Eden, so was blissfully unaware of Lauren being in any danger. Kymmie had taken it upon herself to break into Aunt Jens and make it look as though Lauren had been home. It wasn't unusual for Jen and Lauren to not see each other for days what with Jens hectic work schedule and the fact that Lauren usually spent most of her time out with her friends. The young mystics did worry about how long they would be able to keep up this charade. Only elders had the power to use mind control on a human, and with none of them around to help, their only choice was to do it this way and hope for the best

Kymmie had begun making arrangements for a burial for Jonty. You could tell she was heartbroken, but was trying her best to be strong. Kymmie's grandmother was helping her whilst Jared and Jade worked tirelessly to find out who had taken Lauren. Usually there would be whispers or someone would hear something but this time, nothing.

Jared had travelled two thousand miles North to a town called Ash Meadow and Jade had gone South to a place called Wakes Vale. These towns were similar to Eden; they were homes to mystical beings who lived peacefully within a human community. Kymmie had to stay behind in Eden, she was unable to leave due to her being bound to the spring here, so her job was to wait in Eden for the elders to return and try to keep Aunt Jen from knowing the truth.

Jared arrived in Ash Meadow to meet a friend of the Harvey Family, an elf called Luna Nielson. Luna's father was the leader of the mystics in this town, just like the Harvey's are in Eden. Any settlement must have a leading family who is responsible for the mystic beings in that area. They report directly to elders on all matters involving the safe guarding of humans in their chosen residence.

Jared and Luna had grown up together and had a close bond, Jared had hoped Luna would help him to find Lauren.

Ash Meadow was a quaint village with a population of 907. The buildings in Ash Meadow dated right back to the 18th century, they were built from rubble stone and stone dressed. The country lanes that ran through the village were narrow and windy, only one vehicle could pass in one direction, at one time. Hardly anyone in the village drove, they would mostly have a horse or walk. There was a bus that left from the village on a Monday morning and returned the same day in the late afternoon.

The bus would take passengers to Humber Sands, which was the nearest big town to Ash Meadow. It was the only time the locals would be able to take public transport out of the village.

Humber Sands was comparable to Middle Keynes. It had a big shopping mall, plenty of bars and restaurants and a cinema. It only took around half an hour to drive there from Ash Meadow and nobody seemed to mind that there was only one bus per week. That was just the way it had always been and the locals were not bothered enough to change it.

Jared turned into Nuthall Close, unlike most of the village, this residential area was much newer, the houses were contemporary, built using red clay bricks with tarmacked drives. There were four decent sized houses in the cul de sac and as he pulled up outside, The Nielson property, he noticed Luna already standing on the driveway waiting for him. Luna was a special elf with great psychic powers. She had visions of the future and could see things that were yet to happen and sometimes, she even had the ability to see what had already happened. Luna's powers were rare, she was born under the Crystal Moon of Sion, a spiritual time where the moon changes to look like Crystal Glass.

It is said that this is the window where all realms are interconnected with no walls up to divide them. Energy and vibrations become interlinked and the past and present merge for one single minute. Luna came into this world within those sixty seconds, giving her this special gift.

She stood in front of Jared's car with her head looking down at the floor. Her hair was as white as snow and ran down past her knees. Her skin was of a pale complexion and even her lips were of the palest shade of pink. Jared turned off the car engine and as he did, Luna looked up and into his eyes.

In all the years that he had known Luna, he had never quite been able to get used to her gaze. Luna's eyes were silver, just like two shiny silver coins. Very prominent and mystical to look at. Many humans feared Luna because of the way she looked. Elves had always fitted in with humans because they look like them, only more alluring and pure. Luna looked different, so much so that even some elves were weary of her. She was different and she knew that.

The pair continued to stare at one another until Luna laughed, "You're not still scared of my eyes are you little baby?"

When Jared was a child, he would cry every time Luna looked at him and now every time Luna saw him, she would mock him for it. Jared laughed and got out of the car, "Same old Luna, same old jokes."

They exchanged a hug.

"What can I do for you old friend?"

Luna and Jared began to walk towards the river that ran adjacent to Luna's home. They sat by the water and the two long standing companions spent some time catching up on each other's lives. Jared explained to Luna about Lauren and Jonty,

the abduction and the missing elders.
Luna told Jared that her father had too
been summoned a few weeks back and
she had not heard from him since. She
told Jared that she had not seen anything
that would be of help but assured him
that she would do some magic for him
and try her best to help him find Lauren.

"I love her Luna; I need to find her."

Jared was desperate.

Luna took Jared back to the house, they
walked along the side and entered the
back garden through a side gate. Once in
the garden, Luna led Jared down the
garden path, to an old storm shed
underground. She opened the door and
they both climbed down a few steps into
small dark room. Luna lit some candles
and began burning incense sticks. The old
storm shed had been transformed into a
safe place for Luna to do magic.

The room was very small with only a very low wooden table in the middle, surrounded by big purple and red cushions on the floor. Luna sat down on one side and waved her hand down at the opposing cushions, ushering Jared to sit down. She immediately started chanting and as she did, the candles began to flicker and her open eyes started to glow.

The magic that Luna used was far different to the dark magic the fairies used. The fairies used a magic connected to Demelza. It was evil.

Luna had a rare gift that enabled her to tap into the light magic: the magic connected to Nevaeh. This kind of alchemy was of pure light and love. No harm could come to those who used Luna's style of magic and no harm could be caused with it. Jared sat in silence as Luna connected to the universal powers.

This was a long process and Jared sat patiently for two hours. Luna had suggested to him that he drive home to Eden and that she would contact when she found something, but he did not want to leave without knowing anything, so he waited for Luna to find information for Jared about what had happened to Lauren.

Luna had to connect to the spirit realms and from that place within the universe, she needed to travel through the past, in and out of different energy zones. This was a long process and one that was not always successful. She warned Jared that they could be there for quite some time. Jared was happy to wait. He needed to wait. This was his one true love, he had no choice.

CHAPTER THIRTEEN

Jade had been set with the task of going to Wakes Vale to seek a siren called Almira.

A siren is a mystical woman who enslaves men. When a siren sings, men cannot help but follow her voice. The man becomes powerless and brainwashed. A siren will usually force the man to do an array of tasks for her before finally eating his body. A siren is almost always a very unattractive and aged lady, with a very twisted sense of humour. She is never able attract a man by sight because of her gruesome appearance but her voice can force any male, human or mystical to succumb to her every desire.

Therefore, it had to be Jade who came to see Almira and not Jared, it would be too risky to send Jared for information as Almira might not ever let him leave.

Sirens were created by Demelza, and would normally side with evil, however Jade had a feeling that Kais Kane was behind the abduction of Lauren and she also knew that Almira hated Kais more than anything in the world. He was the one man she couldn't send into trance and this bothered her greatly. Jade hoped that if Almira knew that they were fighting against Kais, she would join them to help take him down.

Being a siren, Almira also had a link to her siren elders. Sirens were the only creatures that had direct psychic links to each other.

If Almira could find out where her elder was then that would tell Jade where her parents were, although this was not going to be easy for Jade.

Sirens had a jealous streak, and with Jade being as beautiful as she was, there was no telling how Almira would react to such a request. Sirens cannot stay in one place for too long, too many missing people in one place tends to draw excessive human attention and their greed always leaves a body count in their trail, which makes it easy for them to be tracked. Jade had followed all the leads she had to Wakes Vale. She had read on a local internet news site that the Priest of this town had gone missing. Prior to his disappearance, locals reported that he had been acting very strangely. According to one devout church goer, Madeline Wilson, the Priest had said that God was in hell and was not coming back to save them.

Jade knew as soon as she read the article that this would be the work of a siren. This is the typical kind of sick game they like to play.

Jade spent the afternoon walking around town and speaking with locals. Wakes Vale was not a very big place, but without an address for Almira, it wasn't so easy for Jade to find her.

Jade was aware that by nature, sirens were nosey creatures, they liked to keep tabs on new arrivals. She thought if she made enough noise with the locals and asked enough questions, people would start to wonder who she was and that would lead the siren to her. So, that is what she did. She questioned everyone she came across throughout the day and then found herself a cheap hotel room just outside of town and waited for Almira to come to her.

The hotel was rundown and remote and most of the rooms vacant. It was the kind of place that attracted humans with bad intentions: cheating husbands and wives, humans who were running from the law and general shady characters who were up to no good in one way or another. Jade chose this place because Almira was unpredictable and she did not want any innocent people to be harmed, should her request for a deal with Almira go sideways.

Jade's room was dull and depressing. The walls were dark olive green and the bed covers were a deep burgundy red. The room smelt like stale cigarettes and bad choices. Jade hated every minute that she waited.

She went into the bathroom, the bath tub was stained and cracked. The light switch was hanging off the wall and the sink taps were covered in rust. Jade rinsed the sink out began splashing cold water on her face, as she looked up at her reflection in the mirror, she jumped. Standing behind her was a very scary looking old lady. It was Almira.

Warts covered her face and thick black hairs grew from these warts in every direction. She had a crooked nose and thin, wiry grey hair.

Jade spun around, but as she did Almira disappeared. Jades face was still wet. She attempted to wipe it dry with the back of the hands as she went into the bedroom, calling out

"Hello?" as she went.

Almira was standing in the bedroom.

"Well now, what brings a pretty little elf to

Wakes Vale, hmmm?"

Almira's voice was deep and husky. She sounded like she had smoked 50 cigarettes a day her whole life. It was hard to imagine that with a speaking voice like hers, she had the ability to sing like an angel. Jade reached over to the bed to pick up a towel to dry her face.

Jade was brave, she was not afraid of Almira. She was an elf with beauty and grace and the heart of a lion.

"I was hoping we could talk."

Jade spoke as she dried her face.

Almira hissed at Jade, she spat

"get out of here now, before I do something, you will regret!"

Jade didn't flinch, she was defiant and calmly repeated.

"I was hoping we could talk, about the Kane family."

Jade had Almira's attention, "Go on, child."

The nosey siren wanted to hear more.

Jade didn't tell her about Lauren or her abduction, if Almira knew that the long-lost daughter of Zenon Valentin was alive and well, she could become unpredictable.

She told Almira about Jonty's murder and that she felt this was the doing of Kais Kane, she told Almira that she believed they were setting a plan in motion to escape imprisonment and that she was needed to help bring them down.

"Kais has made his first move and we need to act now."

Jade had no way of knowing for sure that Kais was involved, she feared he was and knew that she had more chance of Almira helping if she believed, she may have the chance to sing especially for him. At first Almira was uninterested in Jades offer, until Jade reminded her about how much fairies dislike Sirens and how, if the Kane's were successful in battle, the sirens would become a hunted species once again.

"And what is it you require from me, ugly little elf?"

Almira stood with her frail hands clasped together.

"I need to know where the elders are and since you can connect with your elder, you will be able to tell me."

Jade was now standing directly in front of Almira. She did not stutter or tremble. Almira hissed at Jade in an attempt to frighten her.

Evil feeds from fear and Jade was giving Almira no food today!

Almira stood for a moment contemplating her decision. She wanted the fairies gone, once and for all so she finally agreed.

"Get some beauty sleep, my dear, you look like you could use it."

Almira's jealousy was kicking and she snarled at Jade as she looked her up and down.

"I will meet you back here in the morning." And with that, Almira disappeared.

Jade took a deep breath, she was relieved and just needed Almira to stick to her word and turn up in the morning with the whereabouts of the elders, then she could get out of this vile hotel room and back home to help Kymmie.

The night was long and tedious. There was a constant buzzing coming from the light outside the room. The hotel was so run down that pretty much every part of the building was either broken or about to break. Jade could hear two men arguing a few rooms down, their voices were so loud she could hear most of what they were saying. They appeared to be arguing over a woman. Jade tried to turn on the television in her room to drown out some of the sound, but that too wasn't working, so she put on her jacket and went outside to call Jared. She was praying that maybe he had some better news of Lauren's whereabouts. The phone rang for quite some time before Jared answered.

Luna had managed to discover Lauren's rough location; however, her exact whereabouts was cloaked by a spell so, they only had a fifteen-mile perimeter to work with. The good news was that Luna had also seen the van, Lauren was being transported in. So, they at least had a colour and part of the registration plate to go on.

"Me and Luna are driving there now, they have her somewhere in a town called Baxton."

Jade had never heard of this place.

"Do we know who is responsible?"she asked her brother.

"No, some witches, but Luna thinks it's Kais Kane. He has somehow managed to make contact with these witches."

Jade could sense the pain and worry in Jared's voice. She could tell he was trying his best to hold it together, but he was scared. She knew how much Lauren meant to Jared and she knew how far he'd go to save her. Jade told Jared about Almira and they agreed that as soon as she had what she needed from The siren, she too would head to Baxton.

Lauren was like a sister to Jade; she would do anything to ensure the safe return of her brother's soulmate.

~

Back in Eden, Kymmie and her grandmother were making flower wreaths for Jonty's grave and preparing his lifeless body for rest.

By now, there had been more and more whispers pointing to Kais Kane being behind the killing. Mystical creatures everywhere were becoming more and more anxious. Some had even left Eden and gone into hiding far away. Kymmie's grandmother had suggested to Kymmie that they too leave as soon as Jonty had been laid to rest. Kymmie was far too upset to think about anything else right now. She was angry and devastated by her loss, she wanted revenge for her best friend's death and she wanted to help Lauren. She had no idea if Lauren was ok or if she had been harmed or worse killed. She was angry at the elders for not being here to help them. She couldn't understand why at such a crucial time; they would disappear without trace.

The elders were the leaders of each mythical creature. There was one leader for each kind. Zenon Valentin was the leader for elves and before his imprisonment, Kais Kane was the leader of fairies. Below the leaders sat the conglomeration. These were the appointed leaders of different areas around the world. Jared and Jade's parents were the conglomeration of Eden and everywhere South of Ash Meadow. Lunas father was leader of everywhere North of Ash Meadow. The conglomeration were responsible for their kind in those areas and had to ensure that all lived by the rules set by, the elders. The system was set up hundreds of years ago by the prime movers, they came together to unite and find a way for all creatures to coexist peacefully. Before this time, there had been many wars between the kinds and many mystical creatures were being killed, all because they had no mutual grounds to stand upon.

The fairies had always been dirty players within the system and other elders had always had trouble getting them to play by the rules. Kais Kane had rebelled so far in his reign by leading his kind to cause devastation and death everywhere they went.

So, with him being in captivity any fairies who had survived the war had gone mostly into hiding. It would surely be a worry to the elders as too how many of these fairies would resurface should they hear that their leader may soon be freed.

Lauren's arrival in Eden had caused a stir with the elders, so much so, that they ordered all conglomeration to gather immediately. Lauren was never supposed to come to Eden: that much she knew but she could not understand why. Why was she so important? Yeah sure, she was a changeling but there were thousands of changelings in existence and no one worried about them. The truth that Lauren was yet to learn, was she had been born into a prophecy. A prediction so strong that the divine spirits had envisioned her either being the cause of the end of the good world or the demise of the bad world.

Divine spirits were not physical beings; they were universal energies that sent messages to earthly souls. Lauren's destiny had been written in the stars long before she was born so with this in mind, the difficult decision was made to send her away from this life and have her grow up in a normal human town, unbeknown to any magic. No one was to know her whereabouts or have any contact, which was a huge sacrifice for Zenon Valentin. He had no choice but to send her and her mother away. Many of the other elders wanted her life taken from her the moment she was born, but he could not face taking the life of his only daughter. He couldn't put Nicole, the woman he loved with all his heart through something so cruel. Also, when a message comes from a divine spirit, the translation is not always clear. They couldn't take the risk of killing Lauren, in case the prophecy received was unclear. He made the biggest sacrifice all those years ago, Nicole and Lauren were his world and he sent them away for the greater good of the humanity.

Now, here she was, right in the thick of the place they tried to keep her from ever being.

CHAPTER FOURTEEN

Lauren had been in Abigail's basement for two days. She had been hearing lots of chatter from upstairs, mostly from worried teenagers about what would happen should Abigail's parents return home and find Lauren in the basement. It sounded like Kais had not been in contact to give them their next instructions and most were becoming on edge. Lauren had been sat in in the same blood-stained clothes, which had now began to smell awful. To Lauren it was the smell of death. She had not been given any food or water for two days and was severely dehydrated. As she lay on the cold hard floor of the pitch-black basement, she shivered intensely.

Whilst drifting in and out of consciousness, the same few memories replayed over in her mind. The first was the moment Abigail slit Jonty's throat right before her eyes, the second was seeing Jared on the floor in pain, with his eyes rolled to the back of his head. The third memory that replayed over and over was a day from her childhood. Lauren would have only been about five years old, she had been playing in the park with children from her school. One of the children had pushed Lauren from the top of the climbing frame, she rolled down the slide, banging her head on the ground.

As she sat sobbing on the floor with blood running from her wound, she heard a voice in her mind telling her everything will be ok.

This was the same male voice she heard as she crossed into the Safe Haven a few weeks before her abduction. This was a memory that Lauren had long forgotten but for some reason, whilst laying on the floor of the basement in emotional and physical pain, this was the memory she saw over and over.

Lauren eventually lost complete consciousness.

Lauren awoke to having a bucket of cold water thrown over her. As she looked around, she realised, she wasn't in the basement anymore. She was in an old crop barn. Her captors had sat her on an old wooden chair with her hands chained up in her lap. In front of her was a small plastic fold down table, the kind you would take on a camping trip. Lauren had in fact taken one of these camping with her on many occasions. That was before she came to Eden and had got involved with elves and fairies.

Lauren longed for the days when she had a normal, boring life.

She was surrounded once again by witches, only this time, they didn't have their hoods up so Lauren could see their faces. She looked down at her wet body and noticed she was no longer covered in blood. Someone had washed her and put her into a clean change of clothing. Abigail was nowhere to be seen.

"The jeans are Rachel's."

One girl said as she pointed to a chubby blonde girl across the room.

"And the Star Wars t-shirt is Aarons."

Lauren looked over to a young ginger haired boy sat in the corner. He nervously smiled and waved to Lauren.

"Thank you."

Lauren tried to say the words as clearly as she could but her throat so dry and croaky. The girl standing in front of her was tall and slim. Her dark brown hair was long and straight and she wore square framed glasses.

"I'm Beth."

She said, as she threw a tray of food down on the table in front of Lauren. There was a jug of water on the tray and it had spilled everywhere as Beth flung it down. The plate of food was now swimming in a tray of water.

What a bitch, Lauren thought to herself. With her hands, still in chains, Lauren grabbed the jug of water and took gulp after gulp. She then grabbed the food from the plate in front of her and began shoving the food into her mouth like a wild savage beast. It had been days since Lauren had eaten anything. She was starving and did not care what she looked like.

After finishing the food on the plate in front of her, she downed the remaining water left in the jug, but before she could finish it completely, she heard a voice shout, "they're here."

And with that, Beth took the tray and grabbed jug from Laurens mouth and walked away. Moments later the barn doors opened and in walked an older man, dressed in the same cloaks as the others. He was a chubby bald man with a stern facial expression. He had a woman in tow, dragging her along as she tried to keep her footing. She was also in chains. The woman had a cloth bag over her head but Lauren knew immediately that it was Nicole.

"Mum!"

Lauren tried to run to her mother, but her feet were also chained to pillar behind her, causing Lauren to stumble slightly.

"Lauren, baby is that you?"

Nicole couldn't see, so she moved her head around, trying to detect where Laurens voice was coming from.

"Yes, mama its me."

Lauren began to cry out for her mum.

"Let her go!" she screamed. The man chained Nicole to a post on the opposite side of the barn to Lauren, then pulled the cloth bag from her head. Mother and daughter cried together as the witches left the barn, locking the doors behind them. They were too far away to reach each other.

"You are supposed to be travelling the world, where is Dale?"

Lauren saw her mother's face drop. Nicole burst into tears and told Lauren that they never got on the plane.

"These 'kids'- kidnapped us, they killed Dale" she sobbed.

"Why would they do this!"

Lauren could not believe what she was hearing.

"You mean you have been chained up like this all this time?"

How could she not have known? Why didn't she raise the alarm sooner! She had not heard from her mother but assumed she was ok, but she wasn't.

"I am a terrible daughter," she cried.

Lauren told her mum all about what happened in Eden with Jonty. She didn't mention anything about her father being an elf or about any of the other mystical creatures she had met. Nicole had been through enough already; Lauren didn't see the point of confusing her any further.

Lauren told her mother that she had met people who knew her father.

She was hoping that if Nicole knew about him and that she knew that Lauren knew then, she would finally tell her everything, but Nicole just stared at Lauren, like she was searching her mind for missing answers.

"I, I just don't remember him."

Nicole laid on the floor as tears rolled down her face and into the dirt. How could she not remember? Lauren couldn't understand. Her mother had married an elf and she couldn't remember? Lauren could tell that her mother was being genuine, she didn't remember anything about Zenon or what he was. Someone must have erased all her memories of him from her mind, but who would do that?

All Lauren wanted to do, was go over and embrace her mother. After everything they'd had both been through, she just wanted to have her mum put her arms around her and she put hers around her mum. Lauren had a reason to live, to save her mother. Before this moment, she had been so consumed with guilt and self loathe that she had given up fighting, but her mother reminded her that she needed to live and she needed her mother to live.

She needed to find her father and find out why he had left them and why her mother couldn't remember him. From all the stories that she had heard back in Eden about them, they were the world's greatest lovers. No one loved as deeply and unconditionally as they loved one another. In Eden, the locals have a saying for when two people are madly in love, they say… "Oh, those two are Zenicked." Meaning they have fallen so crazily in love: after Zenon and Nicole. Local humans still ask, what ever happened to those love birds? Some actually believe they are still together somewhere, living happily ever after.

She had to reunite her parents and find out why this had happened, she needed to find Zenon and make him explain. Surely, he hadn't forgotten them? Or maybe he had, maybe he too had no memory of Nicole?

Laurens brain was going crazy, all these thoughts flooding her brain. So many unanswered questions.

And where was Abigail? She was meant to be the leader of this cult, but Lauren hadn't seen or heard her for a few days.

CHAPTER FIFTEEN

Kais had summoned Freja, Amara and Benny to his tree house. Up until now, he hadn't shared any of his plans with them but now he was going to tell them what was happening. Freja was still upset that he hadn't confided in her sooner and now he was telling them all at the same time. She felt that she had been more loyal to him than anyone and that he should have included her sooner.

"My witch on the outside is on her way to where the elders are currently gathered, she is delivering a message on our behalf."

Kais spoke to the fairies like a lecturer would a class of students. He strolled around the room as they sat in a line, hanging on his every word. He told them he had Lauren and her mother captured and that the witch was going to offer their release in exchange for the fairies' freedom.

"Are we really going to free them?" Benny questioned.

Kais explained that as soon as they, themselves were freed, he would send word to the witches to kill Nicole.

"Zenon Valentin took your beloved mother from us, now we will repay him with the same favour. The girl will live as she may be of use to us later. With any luck, she'll blame her father for her mother's death and come and join us for revenge"

Kais' words were final. He told them that as soon as they were free, they were to kill all their enemies, every last one of them.

"We will go to battle and take back our freedom and land. Word is being sent to any fairies left in existence, to join us in our fight!"

Kais questioned Amara on her loyalty. He told that he had suspicions about how committed to the family she was.

"I know you had a human boy that you loved and you thought he loved you. He would have long forgotten about you by now, you know, you don't have anyone but us left."

It was true, before imprisonment, Amara had fallen in love with a car mechanic called Daniel Evans. He was a human, no powers, no riches. Just a good and kind man. She had been secretly planning to run away with him. Daniel knew about her being a Fairy, she had finally found someone she could open up to about everything and he still loved her.

He was part of reason that she was so connected to humanity, she knew he wouldn't live forever and that he would grow older much faster than she would, but she wanted to spend the rest of his life with him.

But Kais was could have been right, Daniel would now be a fourty-two year old man, probably married with children and had probably forgotten all about her.

Amara began to cry, her tear scars slowly getting darker and darker.

"Father please stop, her tears are turning black!"

Freja ran to her sister's side to comfort her.

"Father please!!!"

Kais laughed, he was a cruel man.

"If it really was love, then I am sure he has been waiting for you."

And with that Kais walked out the door, slamming it behind him.

Freja tried to calm her sister, not so much because she cared about Amara, but because the sisters were linked. As young fairies, they had often played around with magic they didn't understand. One day they tried a spell that they thought would combine their powers and make them stronger. What they had really done was connect Amaras emotions to Freja's powers. When Amara feels pain and darkness in her heart, her tear shaped scars turn black and she begins drawing power from Freja. Amara could potentially drain Freja of all her powers completely, leaving her as nothing more than a human. If Amara was to drain all of Freja's power, it would be too much for her to contain and would kill her. Freja did not want to be a pathetic human. She wanted to be powerful, therefore she needed to ensure Amara did not become emotionally unstable.

Amara wanted to live so she always tried hard to be positive. Sometimes Kais used to like to play with the girls, by upsetting Amara and threatening Freja with humanity. These were his children, his own flesh and blood, but that never stopped him.

Benny got up to follow Kais. As he did, Amara hissed, "Look at you, running after him, you're not even part of this family. No one even knows where you came from!"

Amara and Freja had always been jealous of Benny, he wasn't Kais' son but Kais had always treated him better than he had his own daughters. This hurt Benny, he didn't know where he came from either so he always tried desperately to feel like a Kane. Kais had told Benny as a child, to never question his background. As far as he was concerned he was one of them and that was that. Benny being the loyal subject of Kais, never challenged it.

Recently though, he had started to feel like he needed some questions answered.

Even though Kais treated him like one of his own, the sisters never did and would often remind him that he was a Ward and not a Kane. He was also a lot stronger than the girls, especially when he was angry, he found he could be even stronger than Kais. This bothered the sisters, especially Freja. She was the first-born Kane, she should rightly be more powerful than any other Fairy her age, but she wasn't.

Benny didn't respond, he didn't even turn around to acknowledge her words. He walked through the door, slamming it behind him.

"I am fed up with Father keeping us in the dark all the time."

Freja was now on her feet, pacing the floor.

"He won't tell us whose kid Benny is, he never told us about this plan to escape this place.

We are his only real family he has left and he just hides everything from us!"

Amara sat without saying a word. She felt the same as Freja, she no longer wanted to be Amara Kane, daughter of the mighty Kais Kane.

No, she wanted to be Mrs Evans, she wanted to marry Daniel and live a happy human life.

But she knew that would never happen, because she was a Kane and Kane's don't get happy endings.

Freja however, did want to be a Kane, she wanted to be 'The Kane.'

She wanted to carry on her father's legacy one day. She was owed that title but she feared that Benny was her competition, especially now Makkalai was dead. Her father had already invested a great deal of time in teaching him everything he knows. Freja wouldn't go down like that, not without a fight anyway.

"Right, that is it! Mar, you keep a look out, I am going to find that spell!"

Freja began rummaging through her father's belongings. Amara walked over to the window, she could see Kais standing by the water's edge looking over at Eden. Benny was stood beside him, just a few steps back. Amara turned to her sister, "Freja, he keeps all of mother's belongings in that old cabinet over there."

Amara pointed to a big set of discoloured and rotting, wooden draws. The chest had eight wide set filing units and the bottom two draws had extensive fire damage to them. There were antique carvings on the sides and the handles looked to be made from steel. Freja hurried over and began riffling through them. Amara continued to watch out of the window. Kais was still by the lake, but now he was showing the communication device to Benny.

"Yes! I found it!"

Amara turned around to see Freja holding a huge grimoire in the air. A grimoire is a book of spells. Every accomplished witch has a grimoire. It is a collection of their work, spells, potions and instructions. You can tell a lot about a witch from her grimoire. Soriah's is one of the most sought after literally pieces in the world. Her extensive knowledge and creations were stored here, it was like the holy bible of magic. The grimoire was bound in the skin from a stingray. The bobbled effect of the material made the book look as though it was covered in tiny black beads. On the front of the grimoire was an emblem carved into the leather. It was the letter D with a sword coming up through the middle from the bottom. The D was a representation of the oath of allegiance that Soriah had sworn to Demelza.

Freja flicked through the pages, looking for the spell of resurrection.

"Freja, you need to hurry, he is coming back!" Freja flicked through page after page until she found it.

"I've got it!"

Freja ripped the page from the book and carefully placed the grimoire back in the drawer. She then cast a quick, spell around the chest of drawers. Kais would be able to sense that someone had been in the drawers, so Freja just covered her scent to make it look as though it was untouched. She folded the piece of paper up and put it down her top. Amara ran back to the middle of the room and pretended to cry, just as Freja reached her sister, Kais opened the door. Freja was comforting her sisters. They had made it look as though they had been there all along.

"You two aren't still moping over some name calling, are you?"

Kais laughed as he walked straight past the girls.

"Get out and find something useful to do." Without even looking at the girls, he just pointed to the door, ordering them to leave. Amara and Freja apologised as they made their way out the door. They gave each a quick look of relief as they did so. Freja had the spell and she could not wait to get off the island and bring back her beloved Makkalai.

~

Jade had fallen asleep on the bed. She had been reading up on witches in Baxter and must have drifted off. She awoke to find Almira standing over her. Jade jumped up.

"Ever heard of knocking!"

Almira had shocked Jade, who was now on her feet and very much awake. Almira laughed, "Well I have, but I didn't feel like it today." Almira chuckled and continued,

"I see the beauty sleep hasn't worked for you, you are still an ugly little elf."

She then just sat down on the bed quietly and just stared at Jade.

"Did you find anything?"

Jade asked, as she tried to break the awkward vibe Almira was creating.

"Hmmm,"

Almira was nodding her head as if to say yes.

"So... where are they?"

Jade was getting impatient now but Almira wanted something from Jade first. She told her that she didn't want to kill Kais, well not at first anyway, she wanted to have him as a prisoner so she could try and figure how he was resisting her powers.

"You will bring him to me, when you capture him. If you don't, I will kill your brother. Oh, and your father as well. Do we have a deal?"

Jade sighed, "Fine, you have a deal."

Jade just wanted to know where the elders were, she would have to deal with Almira's requests later.

"Good! They are in The Valley of Anton."

And with that, Almira disappeared.

The Valley of Anton was a place far way which had a very traumatic history. It had been deserted for years, so Jade had wondered why they would choose this as a place to meet. The Valley of Anton had once been a place that attracted mythical creatures and curious humans from all around the world, due to the natural magic the lands possessed. It was the perfect place to harness magic. You could draw power from the stones and the waters in the pools and waterfalls could heal any wound and in the high moon seasons could even bring a life back from death. As the lands attracted more and more creatures hungry for power, The Valley of Anton started to die. The waterfalls began to run dry and the magic faded. As with anything in life, whatever you take would need to be replenished, which the greedy failed to see.

Over time, The Valley of Anton lost all its magic which resulted in the land becoming baron to the point, you could use no magic at all. Jade was surprised that the elders had chosen a place which they wouldn't be able to use magic at all, even to defend themselves. Here, they were merely humans. Jade called Jared immediately and told him her findings. They agreed that Jared and Luna would continue to search for Lauren and Jade would get a plane to the Valley of Anton to find the elders.

The Harvey family had many connections, one being a guy not far from Wakes Vale.

His name was Bob O'Connell and he was one of the few humans who knew about the Mythical World. He had been a great ally to them over the years. Jade knew he had a plane and that he would be more than happy to assist her.

CHAPTER SIXTEEN

Jared and Luna arrived in Baxter. They had
booked themselves into a hotel in the
middle of town. It was a small family run
place and the owners had lived in the
town for many years, and so they could
share information of the surrounding
areas.

They figured that this would be a good
place to start and work their way out. By
now Jared was barely holding it together.
Thoughts kept running through his mind
of what state Lauren was in. Had she been
hurt? She could be dying and him unable
to save her. He knew that she would be
scared and alone. Would she know how
desperately he was trying to find her? He
just couldn't bear the thought of her going
through this without him by her side
protecting her. Lauren did not deserve
this; she was kind and innocent. Jared
blamed himself for not being able to keep
her safe from dangers like this. He was
being way too hard on himself. No one
had foreseen this, Kais had been

meticulous in his planning over the years and there was nothing Jared could have done differently, but he didn't see it this way. He would give his life if it meant she was safe.

Luna had returned to their room with a map that the hotel owners had given her. She laid the map of Baxter out on a table. She had circled a fifteen-mile radius around their location, so they could clearly see the area in which to search. They knew that Lauren's captors would more than likely take Lauren to a remote area to avoid being seen. Jared then marked all the areas that could be where she was.

Baxter was a big town with not much there, which made the search harder than they had initially thought. They had thirty-six areas of interest marked. Time was of the essence so they wasted no time in setting off to the first place on their map. An old fire station four miles from their hotel, they had a long day ahead of them and were both tired, but they were more determined than ever.

Jade had reached the old farm that Bob O'Connell lived on. He was surprised to see Jade, especially without her parents. He could tell by the way she rushed up to his front porch that something was wrong. Bob was sixty-three years old but strong as an ox. He had lived on this farm his whole life and had been a hunter since a child. He didn't scare easily and locals always described him as a moody old man. He kept himself to himself and rarely socialised with anyone in the town. Bob lost his wife and son forty years ago. They were killed in an 'accident' caused by fairies. He suspected foul play around their deaths and upon delving further discovered the truth about the mystical world around him. This was how Bob and Jade's father came to meet and since then he had done everything he could to assist the elves.

Jade ran to Bob and swung her arms around him. It had been years since she had seen him and he had aged considerably. He had white hair and a white beard. His eyes were hazel and full of spirit behind his now, very wrinkled skin. Jade burst into tears as she told him what had happened.

Of course, Bob agreed to help without question, so he sent Jade into the house to clean up and get some food whilst he got the plane ready. Although locals would never see the kind and caring side to him, that Jade and Jared had always known, it was there. After his family were killed and Bob had learnt the truth, he lost patience with humans and their naïve nature.

He knew of the evil around and vowed to never allow anyone close enough to potentially be a victim, especially as he was on the opposing side to fairies.

Plus, part of him liked being the scary old man that kids would dare each other to 'step on his land.' It made him chuckle when he'd run outside with his shot gun to scare them even more. He would never actually harm anyone but it was a game to him, that he enjoyed playing.

Jade used the bathroom to clean up then headed to the kitchen to make sandwiches for her and Bob. She knew it would be a long day for both and want to ensure that Bob was kept fed and hydrated. He would never admit it but he wasn't as young and fit as he used to be and Jade knew he needed to take more care these days. She packed the food and bottles of water into her backpack and went out to meet him by the plane.

Bob's plane was probably as old as him. He called her Lucille, and she was a white Cessna 172 with blue wings. She carried only two passengers in the front and two in the back. There was not enough room to bring back all the elders and conglomeration, but they would at least be able to bring Jades parents' home to help Jared and Luna. Bob and Jade strapped themselves in and Bob started the engine. Lucille was croaky but Bob assured Jade, she was still fit for the job.

"My Lucille is tough as old boots, so don't you worry 'bout nothing young lady."

With that the plane began to move. As predicted Lucille gained speed and was up in the air in no time. It was a turbulent ride to The Valley of Anton. Jade was so grateful for Bobs help; she would never have made it there without him.

~

In Baxter, Jared and Luna had crossed off six places from their map. They still hadn't found Lauren or any clues to where she would be. They were headed to an old fishing lake, the building there was abandoned. It was another possible place the kidnappers might have taken her. Luna tried to comfort Jared as they drove to the next location. She tried to assure him that Lauren would be ok. She didn't know for sure, in her trance she had seen a lot of death in the coming days, but did not know who the victims would be. She believed that destiny was not decided but merely a predication, each step taken, leading up to an event would change the course. Luna knew they needed to take each step carefully.

"Jared, when we find her, we need to have a plan. If Lauren's abductors were strong enough to stop you last time, they'll be strong enough again this time. We can't help her if we are dead."

Luna and Jared had never practiced combination magic before. It is usually something you learn when the conglomeration leader of your district, feels you are ready for. It is a skill which they teach at the school in the Safe Haven. It can be extremely dangerous for mystical beings to do, untrained. Many elves and fairies have died, horrific deaths because they had no idea what they were doing.

Human witches do not possess the same volume of power, therefore the chances of them consuming too much power to control is highly unlikely.

Luna was worried that in Jared's desperate state, he would fly in, guns blazing and potentially make the situation worse.

Fear for the safety of someone we love can do that, to human or elf or any living being.

They had to be smart and a failsafe extraction plan needed to be discussed and stuck to. She needed Jared to understand this clearly. They had decided between them that when they arrived at each place, they would split up and take different routes. One covering the front entrance and one would cover the back. They would use their mobile phones to communicate and should they see anything, they were to go back to the car to begin surveillance.

From there they would be able to hatch a plan based on how many enemies there were and what exits were available to use.

Each time they approached one of the marked areas, Jared would feel a rush of sickness. He knew each time that this time it could be the place, he could potentially have Lauren in his arms once again in a matter of minutes. They reached the old fishing lake, and as discussed, they split up. Jared and Luna both had earphones so they were able to keep their hands free. Luna went around the back and Jared took the front. Lauren wasn't here and Jared's heart sank.

They went back to the car and both agreed that even though she wasn't there, this was a far better way to conduct their search and quickly moved onto the next location.

~

Jade and Bob had reached The Valley of Anton, as they flew over they both gasped at the beautiful scene below them. Jade had only ever heard stories about this majestic place and how breath-taking it was. Now, she was seeing it with her own eyes and the stories did it no justice. It was stunning. The greenest grass, completely untouched. It hadn't grown wild and unruly, like you would imagine. The waters in the streams were clear blue as it ran through the land, peacefully splashing over smooth granite rocks. They flew over the empty mountains and temples, which years ago would have filled with magic seekers.

The Valley of Anton had blossomed once again. Nature had taken back its beauty and rightfully so. It was the most scenic landscape both Bob and Jade had ever seen. The original Temple of Anton was built thousands of years ago, at the foot of the highest mountain on the west side of the valley. A waterfall ran down the mountain, through the temple, and then out into the sacred pool of life. Jade figured that if the elders were to congregate anywhere, it would be here.

Bob landed the plane as close as he could and the pair made the rest of the journey on foot. They walked through the jungle, just at the edge on the Valley, which unlike the rest of the land, had now wildly overgrown. Bob had brought his hunting rifle with him so insisted on leading the way in case they encountered any mountain lions or any other wild animal that might not be so pleased with their trespassing on their land. With Jade, not being able to use any magic here she was thankful for Bobs hunting experience for protection.

Jade and Bob, arrived on the South side of the fierce, Kongo River. They had to cross a rickety wooden bridge that was very old and unsafe. The panels of wood were held up by rope, but most of the rope lines and footing panels had broken. They crossed one at a time as they knew the bridge would struggle to hold the weight of two.

The crossing had set the pair back, time wise. However, they soon reached the Temple, which was still as magnificent as the day it was built. The doors to the temple were very tall, taller than any normal building would have. They were about as tall as a two-story house in Eden. This was because when it was built, it was built for giants. Nevaeh had built this sanctuary for them to take refuge in, from evil. They had struggled back then for a hiding place from evil, due to their size, so Nevaeh built The Valley of Anton for their protection.

Giants have no magic; they are simply like a human but much bigger. Contrary to what people thought, they were the kindest creatures ever created. The magic here was a gift from Nevaeh to protect them as they had none of their own. After the death of Nevaeh, the land became over run and the giants were pushed out and soon became a hunted species. They had no place to hide and no land of their own.

From the outside, even though the doorway was high, it did not look like the temple itself was very big, but what you could not see from standing outside was that, the sanctorium was situated deep inside the mountain. Hence why, Nevaeh had chosen the biggest mountain. It was large enough for the giants to all take refuge. The wall candles were alight, so Jade knew someone was here.

As they wondered through they noticed drawings and inscriptions carved into the stone walls from floor to ceiling. These were stories of the past, they told of the sadness and the triumphs the giants faced all those years ago.

A nostalgic feeling could be felt as they walked further and further into the mountain. The temple was cold and damp, Jade shivered, the emptiness of the temple sunk through her skin, she thought about Jonty and how his kind had once been safe here.

As Jade and Bob went further in, they could hear echoed voices coming from one of the chambers. They followed the voices as they got louder and louder. The closer they got, the more the voices became recognisable. Jade could hear her father speaking. He seemed to be arguing with someone.

Probably a centaur, Jade thought to herself, they are always being difficult.

Jade pushed the huge carved, wooden doors open. Her and Bob froze, completely still on the spot. Every single conglomeration member of every mythical creature was sat in the tiered seats circling the room. The elders were stood on the floor in the middle. They had all turned to look at Jade and Bob as they stood awkwardly in the doorway.

Robert Harvey, Jade's father immediately got up and rushed towards her. He looked like an older version of Jared, very tall and handsome, with blonde hair. The only difference was his eyes were emerald green like Jade's.

"What is the meaning of this?"

One voice shouted.

"Get them out of here!"

Shouted another.

"Bringing a human in here, how disrespectful!"

There was uproar in the chamber as more and more outraged mythical creatures joined in. There must have been about two hundred creatures at the meeting and all of them were up in arms about Jades intrusion.

"Jade, what are you doing here?"

Robert said as he tried to usher her out the room.

"It's great to see you Bob, but now is really not a good time."

Jade had put her father in a difficult situation by storming into a meeting of elders. It was something that just wasn't done by anyone.

"Father, please."

Jade was trying to explain.

"Not now Jade, you need to go."

He was now still trying to remove Jade from the chamber.

"Zenon please! It's Lauren!"

Jade had now pushed past her father and was looking directly at a man standing in the middle of the room.

The man was tall, just like all elves but there was something different about him, he had an air of authority and power about him that most didn't have. He slowly turned to look at Jade. His hair was long and black with a slight wave. He had a beard, which was rugged but sexy. His physique was muscular and his eyes were piercing blue. He had the smouldering, fierce look in his eyes. There was no doubt about it, he was a very attractive elf. The entire room went silent as the faces stared down.

Not only had Jade interrupted an elders meeting, she had also just addressed an elder without permission. Jade was breaking every rule but she didn't care, she was desperate.

There was a moments silence before Zenon finally spoke, his voice was stern as he told Jade to leave the room.

He then turned his back on her and walked away. Jade's father gave her a disapproving look as he once again ushered her out.

Jade left the room very upset and went to wait outside. She was in a lot of trouble for this, but all she could think about was Lauren and Jonty. Zenon cared deeply for Lauren and was fully aware of the dangers that she was in, but being an elder meant he had to detach himself from his personal feelings for the greater good of all. He could not allow himself to show emotion in front of the people who looked up to him for answers. He wanted to help Lauren and was planning to do so, but he had to do it in a way that abided with the laws his ancestors had made. The laws he had spent his life encouraging others to live by.

To Jade, it looked as though he didn't care, but she was very much mistaken.

Jade and Bob waited outside for what seemed like hours. The meeting had finally called for a break and the conglomeration left the temple and headed off in different directions. They had all set up camps in different parts of the valley. Jade and Bob received a lot of disgusted looks as they walked by.

Jade's father finally emerged. He shook Bob's hand and told him he was happy to see him looking so well.

Her mother, Katherine Harvey, followed shortly after, giving Jade and Bob a hug. Katherine had cherry red hair, which was cut into a neat, graduated bob. Her eyes were flannel grey and when she walked, she did so with a confident and assuring demeanour. It was obvious where Jade got her striking beauty from.

Katherine told Jade to go to the chamber whilst they waited outside. Jade was nervous as she walked back into the temple. It was now empty. Only Zenon was left standing in the huge open room. Jade had read every history book about Zenon, she had always dreamed about meeting him as a child. He was her hero, and over the years, she had aced all of her magic training, in the hopes that one day she could climb the ranks and have the honour of meeting him. Now, here she was, her dream was coming to life... just not in the way that she had hoped.

"I am sorry I barged in, I just..."

Jade didn't get the chance to finish before Zenon stopped her.

"I know you care about my daughter and I am thankful that she has found someone like you."

Jade was relieved, she thought for sure that he would shout or curse at her, serve her an awful punishment. She told Zenon everything that she knew, whilst he stood in silence, listening.

She told him about Jonty and Lauren, the siren and that Jared and Luna were in Baxter looking for Lauren. When she finished, he said nothing. He stood looking at the floor in deep thought. The silence was uncomfortable for Jade, she idolised him but he was now also, the father of one of her best friends. She was unsure how to be around him.

After a while of thought, he asked Jade to follow him. He led her out of a door at the back of the chamber and down some narrow winding steps, to what looked like a dungeon of some sort. It was dark and damp with mould growing on the walls. Jade was nervous.

They stopped outside a wooden door which was bolted shut. Zenon turned to

Jade and told her that there was much she didn't know. He made Jade promised not to let anyone know that he was showing her this.

"The others are already outraged by you being here, you must pretend you know nothing." Jade agreed.

"You have my word."

Zenon unbolted the door and pulled it open. As Jade looked in she saw a young girl sitting in the corner of the room. It was Abigail.

He told Jade that Abigail was the one who killed Jonty and took Lauren. He told her that she was right to believe that Kais Kane was behind it. He had used Abigail to carry out his devious plan and then sent her here to bargain for the fairy's freedom. Jade was horrified as she stood looking at her friend's killer. This now, helpless young girl had murdered an innocent changeling in cold blood.

Jade lunged towards Abigail, screaming at her to tell them where Lauren was. Zenon grabbed Jade and pulled her from the room, closing and bolting the door behind him.

"She does not know where they are. The other witches have moved them to a different location, Kais knows what he is doing." Zenon now had his hand on Jades shoulder.

"Them?"

Jade was confused, "they only have Lauren... don't they?"

Zenon bowed his head in despair, he told her about Nicole and that Kais had demanded their freedom and if it was not given, they would kill Nicole in front of Lauren in the worse way possible. Then, Lauren would be next.

He told Jade that Kais knew he nor any other elf, would never let that happen and the meeting of elders was for them to find a way to control the situation with little or preferably, no casualties.

Some were saying let them die, some were saying save them. The structure of the elders was a democracy, intended to make sure everyone was happy with the choice made.

Or at least a majority. As it stood right now, no one was agreeing.

The next steps were to trial Abigail for her crimes. Zenon explained that later this afternoon, she would stand in front of the elders and her fate would be decided.

"There is a good chance, she will be sentenced to death."

Jade could tell that it pained Zenon to say these words. He vowed to love and protect all humans and it saddened him to see that this one had fallen so far into evil.

Zenon told Jade to go back to her parents and await instructions from him. He told Jade he would keep her in the loop but it had to be done quietly. She agreed and left. Jade could clearly see for herself, why so many looked up to him. Although he was scary, he was also very fair and wanted the best for everyone, he was a true leader.

CHAPTER SEVENTEEN

Jared and Luna had now marked off twenty unsuccessful locations. They were both tired and frustrated, but tried to remain positive.

"OK, next on the list. An old barn off Ridge Oaks."

Luna tried to add some bounce in her words to keep the momentum going.

According to the search engine on her phone, 'the land was brought by some investors to build on, but the construction never took place because of a petition from locals.'

Luna had been researching each place on her mobile phone prior to arrival.

Technology these days enabled you see pictures and gather information with the click of a button. This was helping them with their search.

"It should be just up here on the right."

Luna pointed out of the window to a big red barn across the field.

"Luna, that is quite a lot of vehicles outside for a place that is meant to be abandoned."

Jared turned to Luna, realisation that this might be it, crossed their faces.

"Pull up behind those trees."

The barn was in an open field. They wouldn't be able to drive up without being seen. One of the adjacent fields had corn growing in it. The corn was high, so they would be able to sneak up undetected by foot. They got out of the car and crawled through some bushes to get a better look.

They had both came equipped with binoculars and were looking at the barn. There were a few witches standing outside the building. Jared recognised them immediately by their cloaks.

"That's them!"

He whispered to Luna.

"She is in there!"

- "We need to wait a while and see how many there are."

Luna could tell Jared was eager to get in there but they had to make sure they had a plan first. After a while, it was decided that the three witches out front must be the only ones. There may have been more inside but no one had gone in or out so they would have to take a chance. Jared was to take the corn fields and sneak up to the barn, they would recognise him so he had to stay hidden. If they were to see him then the whole thing would be over.

To the side of the barn was a hatch door, he would need to quietly open the hatch and get inside. Once in, he would free Lauren and sneak out the way he came in.

Luna was the distraction. They wouldn't know who she was so it was up to her to walk up to the barn and pretend to be lost. Luna had a distinctive look, so Jared told her to tie up her very long hair. He then gave her an old baseball cap he had in his car for her to put on and some aviator sunglasses to cover her silver eyes. Luna rolled up her shorts so that they were nearly showing her bum cheeks. She needed to look like a human country girl and she noticed that two of the three witches were male. Showing some flesh would be good distraction tactics. This was it.

They were going to save Lauren.

It was all going to plan. Jared had snuck up to barn through the corn fields and had climbed through the hatch. Luna was wandering down the dirt road, acting like she was lost.

"Oh hey!"

She called and waved to the witches standing outside.

"Can you tell me how to get back to town?" The male witches stared at Luna with their mouths open, then looked at each other. Beth walked over towards her.

"No, we aren't from round here either, but this is private property, so you need to be going." Beth was unimpressed with Luna's damsel in distress act.

"Oh ok, I'm sorry. I don't suppose you have any water, do you? It's hot and I've been walking around for ages."

Luna just needed to keep them distracted for a few more minutes. She hoped Jared was in and that nobody was guarding inside.

Beth rolled her eyes at Luna, she was a miserable cow. Luna smiled sweetly, "If you don't mind."

And so, Beth begrudgingly walked over to one of the vans parked outside.

The two guys didn't take their eyes off of Luna, so she decided to play up for them by bending down to fix her laces.

Seduction was not one of Luna's usual traits, in fact, it made her feel rather uncomfortable, portraying herself as a sex object.

There was a lot at stake for the young mythicals; so today she swallowed her insecurities and played up for the boys.

Jared was in the barn, he looked around. There were no witches in sight. He ran over to Lauren who was asleep on the ground, still chained up. He woke her up and told her to stay quiet. Lauren burst into tears, she was so happy to see him.

"You have to free my mum."

Lauren pointed over to her mother laying on the ground on the other side of the barn.

Jared was shocked, he had no idea that Nicole was in there too. This wasn't in his plan, he hoped he could still get them both out... alive. Jared held his hands over the chains on Laurens wrist, closing his eyes and using his magic, the chains opened. He did the same to the ones on her feet. Once Lauren was free, she ran over to her mother and threw her arms around her.

"Mama, this is Jared, he has come to save us." Nicole was confused and de-hydrated. Jared did the same with Nicole's chains, whilst telling them, "You both need to be very quiet and do exactly what I say if we are going to get out of this barn."

Nicole was in a bad way; she couldn't stand up. Weeks and weeks of neglect and food and drink deprivation, had left Nicole seriously in need of medical attention. Jared gave Lauren his backpack to hold and lifted Nicole up off the floor. He told Lauren to climb through the hatch first and run to the corn field.

At first Lauren was hesitant to leave without her mother. Jared assured her he would follow closely behind with her mother, but she had to go now, before anyone suspected anything. She climbed through the hatch and ran as fast as she could to the corn field.

Next was Jared, he struggled to get through the hatch with Nicole in his arms. She was falling in and out of consciousness and completely oblivious to what was happening around her. Jared wobbled and the hatch nearly slammed down as he went through, Jared just managed to stop the door hitting the wooden frame with his foot. If he hadn't managed to stop the door slamming, they'd have been caught.

Luna saw Lauren run past. Beth had retrieved a bottle of water from the van and was bringing it over to Luna. The witches were all facing Luna and had no idea what was going on behind them. As Beth passed the bottle to Luna, Luna saw Jared run from the barn into the corn fields carrying Nicole.

"Be on your way now," Beth said. Luna was relived, they were out.

"Thank you for your kindness."

She said as she turned to walk back towards the trees. Luna was shaking with adrenaline and fear, she just needed to get back to car as quickly as she could without looking suspicious.

Jared told Lauren to run ahead in a straight line as fast as she could, he told her not to stop until she reached the trees. He ran behind her still carrying Nicole, who was now completely unconscious again. Lauren ran as fast as she could towards the trees, it felt like she was running but getting no closer. Her legs were shaking beneath her, they were going numb and just as she reached the trees, her legs gave way and she began to fall.

Someone caught her. As she looked up, she saw two diamond eyes stare down at her, it was Luna. She helped Lauren into the front seat of the car. Jared was close behind, he gave Luna a 'thank you' look as he placed Nicole onto the backseat. Luna climbed in the back on the other side, she had a bottle of water ready to give to Nicole.

Jared got into the car and started the engine, he looked at Lauren and wanted so badly to take her in his arms. But he had to get them as far away from the barn as possible. He put his foot down on the accelerator and drove as fast as he could, until the red barn in his rear mirror had completely, disappeared.

Lauren was shaking, so Jared leaned over and took one of her hands and held it until the quivering stopped. He had his girl and she was safe. Lauren looked over at him and smiled. He had risked his life to save hers. Lauren felt like the luckiest girl in the world having the unluckiest time.

CHAPTER EIGHTEEN

Abigail stood before the elders.

It was extremely rare to see an elder, they stayed hidden away most of the time.

Not Zenon nor the elder of kappa had been seen since the fairies' imprisonment. There were eight of them, eight leaders of eight different mythical creatures. A siren, centaur, goblin, bogle, nymph, kappa, mothman and Zenon, an elf. There was no leader for giants or gnomes, as both of these creatures had become almost extinct, so any remaining creatures of these kinds, fell under the watch and protection of the elves. The centaurs were half man, half horse. They were great fighters, that had roamed the earth, for centuries. They would usually wander from place to place alone, seeking new adventure. Centaurs did not harm humans and were not evil creatures. However, they were considered to be very grumpy

and short-tempered. Which is probably
why they travelled alone.

Goblins were horrible little creatures,
always dirty and smelly. They lived for
gold and spent their days stealing
anything valuable or shiny from humans.
Most had flocked to the sewages in big
cities. None of the other mythical
creatures had any time for them, but
there were a lot of goblins alive, so they
had to have an elder and be included in
the meetings, if nothing more but to keep
tabs on them.

The bogles were more demonic spirits
rather than creatures. You could see
them, they would shape into something
that resembles a human figure, then they
would quickly disappear and reappear
again. They fed from fear, so their survival
came from haunting humans. Although
they never intended to kill, sometimes,
they would scare a human to death. These
incidents never went down well with the
elves.

Then there were the mothmen, winged creatures in the form of a man, they had red eyes that hypnotized their victims, sending them into an eternal trance. No one liked the mothmen and the mothmen didn't like anyone else, in fact they didn't even like each other.

The kappa elder ruled the Freshwater clans and the Salters. Although, most of the Salters lived deep within the oceans and had no contact with any other creature anyway. He mostly had to keep an eye on the clans that resided close to the shores, but on the whole, they were mostly left under the ruling of a group of outlaw Salters, that lived in the depths of the Indian Ocean.

Abigail was full of remorse. She cried and begged forgiveness, she told the congregation of elders that Kais had persuaded her it was the right thing to do, she had no idea that the fairies were evil. The elders sympathised, they believed she was sorry for her actions and had been yet another a victim of the fairies scheming. They agreed to let her go, but on the condition that her memory be wiped clean of all mythical existence and she was forbidden to do magic ever again.

~

In Fey Forest, Kais had told Benny, Freja and Amara to get ready. He told them to pack anything they wanted to take and to meet him at the water's edge.

"The elders will never agree to freeing us, Father has gone crazy."

Amara was standing in Freja's doorway watching her sister pack her belongings.

"Mar, you should be doing as he says and not standing here bothering me."

Freja was short with her sister. Freja knew what her father was like, he would never tell them to pack their stuff if he wasn't certain of the outcome. Amara wasn't taking his words seriously. The elders would never agree to his demands and he must know that they wouldn't be able to keep the girl and her mother hidden forever. Someone would find them and free them and then they'd have nothing to trade with. Even if Zenon wanted to make the deal, the others would never agree to it.

The elder of the kappa had placed the spell over the island 18 years ago and only he would be able to reverse the spell. The kappa does not care for humans or elves or any other creature for that matter, except their own. He would never agree to it. He knows that if the fairies were to be freed, the first creatures to be exterminated by the Kane's would be the kappas, Freshwaters and Salters.

"Mar, if you want to stay, fine. Just leave me alone."

Freja pushed her through the door and slammed it in her face.

"Fine! I'll go along with this madness; it's not like I have anything better to do!"

She begrudgingly went back to her tree house to start packing.

Amara was the last to join the fairies down by the water's edge. She dropped her bags on the floor and sighed as they waited, looking over at the shores of Eden in anticipation.

~

Abigail sobbed and thanked the elders for their kindness. She promised she would never do any magic again and wanted nothing more than to return home to her family. She reached out to the elder of the kappa and asked him for a tissue. He walked over to the table beside him and pulled a tissue from the box.

Then, he walked back over to Abigail and handed it to her. As he did so Abigail pulled out a sharp knife she had hidden up her sleeve and drove it through his head. Before anyone could do anything, she pulled the knife from his head and took the blade to her own throat.

They both fell to the floor.

The elders were utterly shocked; their blood ran cold. They had not been expecting anything like this to happen. Abigail had played them; this was the plan all along and they hadn't realised. Of course, they wouldn't agree to releasing the fairies, Kais knew this. He set this up to kill the kappa who cast the prison spell.

Kais knew that if he was to die, the spell would be broken and they would be free.

Usually, if an elder is close to death, their successor is always ready and waiting to cast all existing spells. In the past, the exchange of ruling has always been fast and smooth running, but this untimely death meant they wouldn't have time to re-cast a spell, before The Kane's could escape. His plan had been executed perfectly. Abigail had fulfilled her mission and taken her own life once she had completed it. Panic filled the room.

The spell was broken.

The fairies were free.

~

There was a huge bang in Eden. Blue lights lifted from the waters, like fireworks.

The fairies felt a rush of energy fly past them. Kais turned to his children smiling.

"Let's go."

CHAPTER NINETEEN

There was panic amongst the elders back in The Valley of Anton. They knew that the death of The kappa elder would have lifted the spell and they would be too far away from Eden to do anything.

They had gathered the conglomeration back into the temple to give them the news of what had happened. No one had anticipated this outcome. They had spent weeks trying to determine what Lauren's arrival to Eden would entail and the past few days negotiating how to proceed with Kais Kane's demands.

They had completely over looked the fact that The fairies may have been playing a far more devious game.

The remaining conglomeration of kappa were devastated by the news that their leader had been murdered, they worried for the safety of their kind back in Eden. Due to them being in a no-magic zone, they couldn't send word back to Eden to warn them of the impending danger. Jade had tried to use her mobile phone, but The Valley of Anton was so far away from any human civilization, that she had no service to make the call. She needed to get word to Jared, now that the fairies were free, they would make executing Lauren and her mother a priority.

Jade feared that if they hadn't already saved her then they would now more than likely be too late.

The chamber was in uproar. The mythical creatures were frightened and the meeting was spiralling out of control.

"SILENCE!"

Zenon stood in the middle of the room. The entire room, stopped still. No one said a single word. Zenon was the only one strong enough to calm the mythicals and lead them into battle.

"I stand before you as the leader of elves and an ally to you all. Today we lost a dear friend and that saddens me deeply."

Zenon walked around the room, looking at all as he spoke.

"But his death must not be in vain, we must fight this, together as we always have. Our brothers and sisters in Eden are now in grave danger and we must go to them as one!"

As Zenon spoke, his words became louder and stronger. He was rallying the troops as a true leader would.

"We must fight them as one!"

Zenon now had one fist in the air, punching as he spoke.

"And we will bring peace back to our lands once again and live as one!"

The entire chamber was now on their feet cheering and stomping.

"As one!" they shouted.

"We leave for Eden immediately!"

Zenon marched from the chamber and out of the temple as his troops followed closely behind. Once outside, Zenon called for Jade's father.

He told him that he and Jade were to go ahead with Bob and find Lauren, whilst he led the others to Eden to try and stop the fairies.

Bob, Jade and her father ran ahead, into the jungle and towards Lucille.

They reached the old bridge that crossed the Kongo River. It was late in the day and the wind had grown stronger, causing the bridge to rock from side to side.

Bob went across first and as he carefully took step after step, the bridge started to make loud creaking sounds. Just as he reached the edge, he almost lost his footing when he placed one foot one a flimsy, unstable board. Bob grabbed the ropes on either side of him and lunged forward, landing safely on the soft grass. He felt a wave of relief as he took a deep breathe.

Jade went next, she moved quickly and lightly, like a feather floating in the breeze.

Last to cross was Jade's father, he was lot heavier than the other two, Robert knew that he had to go last, because there was more chance of him causing further damage to the already weakened and fragile crossing. Robert moved slowly, each board he stepped upon, made an unnerving splitting sound. The rope behind him started to fray. Jade shouted to her father to hurry. Robert turned to look behind him, he knew the rope would not hold him, but he had to get home, he had to save his son and the people of Eden. Robert, closed his eyes and breathed deeply. He counted to three and ran as fast as he could, the rope snapped and the bridge fell on one side. Robert was now hanging onto a board as the bridge dangled tenderly.

"Father, climb up!" Jade was terrified, as she desperately called down to her father. Robert began to climb up the bridge as if it were a ladder, the boards were breaking off with the weight of his feet, as he eagerly tried to make it to the top. Bob reached over the edge and held his hand down to Robert.

"Grab my arm Robbie, I'll pull you up."
Bob had been one of the very few people
who called Jades father Robbie.

Jade was crying, she was so worried about
her father, the bridge was falling apart
and was moments away from completely
collapsing. Robert looked down, he could
see the angry current below him, crashing
and rolling like thunder. If he fell, he
would never survive. The water would pull
him under and drag him miles down the
river. Robert looked up and saw Bobs
hand, he climbed as quickly as he could.
The last rope holding the bridge up slit
and just as the bridge fell, Bob grabbed
Robert's arm and pulled him up. Jade
threw her arms around her father and
sobbed in relief.

"We have to keep moving." Robert was
now on his feet and leading the others
through the jungle. Lucille was insight,
they began to run towards the plane.

Once in the air, Jade took out her phone and waited for a signal. It had seemed like forever before that 'one bar' popped up on the screen of her mobile phone. Jade dialled her brothers number, she felt sickness in the pit of her stomach as the call rang. Jared finally answered the other end, Jade was thankful to hear that Lauren and her mother were safe. Jade told Jared what had happened in The Valley of Anton and how Abigail had killed the kappa which lifted the curse. She warned him not to go back to Eden as it was unsafe. Jared and the others were now, just outside Eden. They were about five miles away. Jared pulled over on the side of the road to discuss what Jade had told him with the others.

"We can't turn around Jared, what about Kymmie and Aunt Jen. I won't leave them there!" Lauren was adamant that they too must fight. She told Luna to take her mother and the car and find some place safe to stay. Lauren and Jared were to go the rest of the way on foot to find Kymmie and her Aunt Jen. Jared wasn't prepared to argue with Lauren, she was stubborn because she cared for others and this was one of the reasons he fell in love with her. He knew the woods around Eden better than anyone so he and Lauren got out of the car and began to cut through the trees. They had planned to go to Kymmie's first as she lived deeper into the forest, so they would have to pass her to get to town. Lauren hoped that Aunt Jen was out of town today. Her house was so close to the lake, that Lauren was certain she would be in the greatest danger.

As they reached Kymmie's home in the woods, they noticed that the front door of the cottage was open. Lauren and Jared crept up to front door and quietly called out for Kymmie. There was no answer. Jared told Lauren to stay put as he went in to investigate. The cottage had been turned over. The tables and chairs had been overturned and the ornaments and pictures had been smashed on the floor. As Jared walked into the kitchen he saw Kymmie's grandmother, laying on the floor. She was dead, her heart had been ripped from her chest. Lauren had not listened to Jared when he asked her to stay outside. She screamed when she saw the elderly lady, lifeless and brutally murdered in her own kitchen. Jared pulled Lauren towards him and tried to shield her from the body.

"I told you to wait outside!" Said Jared.

Lauren was shaken. "Where is Kymmie?"

After searching the cottage and finding that Kymmie was nowhere to be seen, they left Kymmie's home. Lauren was still in shock from what they had both just witnessed. They headed to Jonty's shack. They figured if Kymmie was not at home, then she could have been hiding out there. Lauren and Jared, took each step carefully. They moved as quietly as they could, knowing that the fairies might still be around. When they got to Jonty's old shack, they saw a huge tree had fallen and had completely crushed the already fragile wooden hut. As they neared, they could hear a voice calling for help. It was Kymmie. The tree had fallen on to the shack and had covered the trap door that had led to the basement. Kymmie was alive, but she was trapped. In hindsight, this had probably saved her life. Had she been out in the open, the fairies would have killed her without question.

Jared used his powers to lift the tree from the ground, white lights emancipated from his hands as the giant-sized tree levitated up into the air and across the ground. Now they could open the hatch and free her. Lauren looked on in awe. Even through all the devastation around her, she couldn't believe she had a boyfriend who could do magic like this. Jared lifted the hatch and looked down to see Kymmie's happy and smiling face staring up at himand his heart sank.

"Boy am I glad to see you!" Kymmie reached up, as Jared pulled her out. Kymmie stood up and dusted herself off. She had no idea what had happened.

"I was looking for Darrig and I guess a storm must have blown the silly old tree down." Kymmie ran over to Lauren and threw her arms around her friend. "I am so glad you are ok!" Jared and Lauren looked at each other, they knew Kymmie did not know that the fairies were free, they had to tell her what was happening.

"It, it wasn't a storm Kymmie," Lauren was hesitant.

"Ha, don't tell me it was one of Jared's magic tricks gone wrong, when he was trying to impress you, Lauren." Kymmie was chuckling to herself as she poked at Jared.

"Actually, Kymmie Lockett, it was you who set the classroom on fire in year seven, with crap magic tricks." Jared was now poking back at her and the pair laughed together. Lauren smiled, she was thrilled to see them both joking around, but she had to tell Kymmie, what was happening around them. "Kymmie, something happened and, and," Lauren stammered at first but as she went on the words quickened, "now the fairies are free."

"THE FAIRIES ARE WHAT?" Kymmie was not expecting that response.

"Please," she pleaded to her friends, "My grandmother! We have to get to her and tell her!" Laurens heart sank as she broke the news of her grandmothers, untimely death to Kymmie.

Lauren could see the words breaking Kymmie's heart as she fell to ground. Her cries filled the forest. She had lost her best friend and her grandmother in the space of a week. Lauren burst into tears as she ran over to comfort the delicate and broken, little nymph, who was crying and sobbing into the dirt.

"I am so sorry Kymmie, I am so sorry!" Lauren had her arms around her fragile friend, trying her best to console her. To lose so much in such a short space of time, Lauren couldn't even imagine feeling what Kymmie was going through. She promised Kymmie that she would help her to get her revenge. "They will pay for what they have taken, I promise you."

"I should have listened to her, my gran told me we should leave and I didn't listen and now... now she is dead!" Kymmie sobbed on Laurens shoulder. Jared gave the girls a few minutes together before helping them both from the floor, he told them that they needed to keep moving as it was not safe to stay. The three of them continued to walk towards the town. They soon reached the centre of Eden. Usually, at this time of day, it would be busy. People would be finishing work or the children would have returned to Eden on the school bus from the neighbouring town; they would be making their way home to family or out with friends. Lauren, Jared and Kymmie had walked into the aftermath of a brutal killing spree. It was quiet, bodies of humans and mythicals alike, littered the streets. Children had been killed whilst they played in the park and the school bus stood in burning flames by the side of the road. The fairies had taken the lives of every living thing in their path. No one had gotten out alive. As they made their way to Aunt Jens, they saw hundreds of kappa, floating dead on the lakes waters. It was the most horrific scene any of them had ever witnessed. The fairies had wiped out an entire town within minutes: all unsuspecting victims, going about their business with no knowledge of what evil was lurking in the trees of Fey Forest.

Lauren ran into Aunt Jens house, calling her name, praying that she wasn't hurt. Aunt Jen was not there. Lauren saw a note on the table in the front room.

Lauren, I am sorry I haven't been around much, we have been like two ships passing in the night. I will be away for the next few days, but I promise, when I come home, we will spend some time together! Please be safe, chilli in fridge for dinner. Love Jen
x

Lauren was relieved to see that Jen had been out of town. She just prayed that the note was recent.

CHAPTER TWENTY

Lauren and Kymmie went to Jared's house to wait for Jade, whilst Jared headed back to Kymmie's house. Kymmie did not want her grandmother's body left to rot on the floor of their home. Knowing that Kymmie wouldn't be able to handle seeing her grandmother in this way, Jared had offered to go on her behalf.

The fairies had cut all the power lines in Eden, so Lauren and Kymmie collected up as many candles as they could.

It was now getting dark as they sat in the dimly lit living room, neither of them knew what would happen next, they were frightened and grieving for the towns devastating loss.

There was an eerie feeling in the night air. Lauren apologised to Kymmie, "I am so sorry for what happened to Jonty, it is all my fault."

Kymmie rushed over to sit by Lauren and put her arms around her.

"Lauren, this is not your fault."

Lauren brushed Kymmie's arm off told her exactly what had happened, she told Kymmie that Abigail had threatened to kill one of them and that she had ignored her threats, she continued to tell Kymmie, how if she had just gone with them when they first asked, they would not have killed Jonty and that he would be here with them now.

Kymmie pulled Laurens shoulder around, forcing Lauren to look directly at Kymmie...

"Lauren, this is not your fault! You do not know the fairies, you have no idea what sick games they play. They would have killed Jonty regardless. YOU ARE NOT TO

BLAME!"

Lauren leaned into Kymmie and the pair hugged and sobbed.

The silence was broken as they heard the front door open and the two girls jumped up in panic.

"It could be Jared."

Kymmie whispered. Lauren knew that Jared wouldn't have returned that quickly. They pair ran and hid behind the sofa. They heard the door to the lounge open...

"Hello?"

It was Jade.

Overwhelmed with relief, Lauren and Kymmie jumped out from behind the sofa and ran towards their friend. Lauren threw her arms around Jade and held her tightly. Standing behind Jade was Jades father. They had left Bob back at his farm. Bob had wanted to come along, but Jade's father insisted that he stayed as it was too dangerous and they may need his help later, but they would need him to be alive.

"Lauren, this is my father, Robert Harvey." Jade moved aside as her father stepped forward and offered his hand to Lauren.

"It's an honour to meet you Miss Fisher, I wish the circumstances were different."

Lauren and Kymmie told them what they knew, Lauren had pulled Jade aside to tell her about Kymmie's grandmother and that Jared had gone to get her body. Jade and her father had already witnessed the devastation as they drove into town, but the darkness had hidden much of the terror. Jade told them that the elders were on their way to help, yet they had no plan of action because no one really knew what was going on.

"Lauren, your father is on his way here."

Jade's words were tender. Lauren was nervous and apprehensive. This is what she had always wanted - to meet her father, but not like this. She had always envisioned what it would be like, it would be a joyful reunion, they would hug and laugh and he would have a good reason for leaving her. But instead, she would be meeting him in town which hours earlier, had fallen victim to mass murder. Mass murder caused by fairies! Lauren had read many fairy Tales as a child, but none of them were like this.

Lauren had taken a shower at the Harvey's and was in Jared's bedroom drying her hair. It felt good to wash the last few days from her skin. She had been starved, thrown down the stairs and chained up like a dog. She began to think about her poor mother and the terror she had been through. Lauren thought that a few days was bad, but her mother had been locked up for weeks and with Lauren watching Jonty being killed, Nicole had to watch her own husbands murder. Her thoughts were interrupted by a knock on the bedroom door. She hoped it would be Jared but assumed it would be Jade or Kymmie.

The door opened and Lauren turned around. She froze as she stared at the man standing in the doorway.

He was tall and handsome with eyes as blue as the ocean. Lauren knew immediately that this was her father. She sensed it immediately.

"Hello Lauren"

That voice, Lauren recognised his voice. It was the same voice that comforted her as a child when she fell from the slide, the same voice that spoke to her in Latin at the Safe Haven.

"I am your..."

Zenon did not get a chance to finish his sentence. There was an almighty bang from outside. They could hear screaming and shouting. A ball of fire shot through the bedroom window, just missing Lauren as it flew past.

"Come quickly, we need to get you some place safe!"

Zenon gently guided Lauren out of the bedroom and down the stairs.

"Robert, take the girls out the back way and get them somewhere safe!"

Zenon ushered the girls towards the back door, before rushing out the front and disappearing into the dark night.

That was it, that was the moment Lauren had waited her entire life for and all she got was a moment to look at him and an unfinished sentence. There were explosions happening all round and she could hear screams and voices shouting for help. Lauren knew that she could be killed tonight and would never get the chance to know him. She was angry at the fairies for everything! They killed her friend and step-father, tortured her mother, destroyed her new home and now, they had taken away her special daddy reunion.

"What is happening?"

Lauren asked.

"The fairies are here; we have to go."

Jades father led the girls out the back and into the woods. He told them to run as fast as they can towards the Safe Haven.

Eden was in the midst of an epic war for the second time today. News of Kais being freed had travelled and just as the elders had feared, fairies from all around had come out of hiding to join him in the fight. They wanted revenge and more than 300 of them had arrived in Eden to fight for their lord, Kais Kane.

Most of the goblins had decided to run and hide, which didn't surprise anyone. The reason they were still in existence was because they hid away like cowards all the time. Sirens were seen feasting on their enemy's flesh on roadsides. Almira had found her way to Kais, she was so hell-bent on getting her dirty long finger nails into him, that she acted foolishly. She ran towards him, hissing and snarling, Kais had seen her coming and raised his hand up in the air, then with one fierce downward movement; he split her body clean in half. She was only a few metres

away from him, when her now separated
body fell apart on crashed onto the floor.

Kais laughed.

Elsewhere, centaurs were shooting arrows
into the darkness. Their aim was
impeccable and they never missed a shot.
Many nymphs and mothmen had been
slayed by the fairies, they weren't as
strong as some of the other creatures, but
they fought as hard as they could and
their bravery did not go unnoticed.

The heavens opened and torrential rain
poured down from the skies. Thunder and
lightning crashed through the air, mixing
in with the bangs and flashes of the fight.
The rain fell, carrying the blood with it as
ran down the streets like a red river.
There was an awful smell in the air,
Lauren wasn't sure if the smell was the
dead bodies, the remnants of magic or the
smell of fear. The reality was, it was a in
fact a mixture of all those things.

The bogle spirits had not joined the elders in battle. They felt their allegiance should be with the fairies but agreed to stay out of this battle as a neutral party. Screams of pain could be heard through the woods. Blood, soaked the ground, Eden was the worst place to be in the world on this soon to be historical night.

A mothman stood hypnotizing Freja, his red eyes locked on hers, she was in a trance. She was foolish to get so close to him, her powers were not as strong as they had once been. Being imprisoned all these years had left her feeling weaker than she would have eighteen years ago. The mothman walked closer to her with an axe in his hand. She was powerless to move. The mothman raised his axe in the air ready to swing it into the side of Freja's head, when all of a sudden, he stopped still and dropped the weapon to the ground. Benny had come behind him and put his hand through the back of the unsuspecting mothman's head and ripped his eyes right out. The trance link broke and Freja watched as the he fell to the ground, revealing Benny standing behind him holding two red eyes glowing in the palm of his hand.

Benny cheekily smiled at Freja, to which she rolled her eyes and stormed off in a huff. She was angry at herself for being caught short, but to then have to be saved by Benny Ward of all people, just made her furious.

"What? Not even a thank you!"

Benny called out to her as she disappeared into the trees. Zenon watched Benny from behind a tree, he had many opportunities to kill Benny but he didn't. He followed him, simply observing his every move.

CHAPTER TWENTY-ONE

It was dark in the woods and Lauren could barely see in front of her, she ran and ran until she had run out of breath. She slowed down and realised she was alone in the woods. She had somehow gotten separated from the others.

She was lost, as she stood and looked around her. She did not know which direction she had come nor which way she should run.

As she spun around, trying to see through the trees, she got the feeling she wasn't alone.

"Is anyone there?"

Lauren called out.

She heard a man laugh.

It was Benny.

He emerged from the trees, taunting her.

"A weak little Changeling like you shouldn't be out in the woods on her own."

Benny was moving around so fast. One minute he was in front of her, then behind her. Each time he appeared he was standing closer and closer to her until.

WHACK!

Benny hit Lauren with the back of his hand so hard that she flew across the ground, hitting her head on a tree.

Lauren tried to sit up as blood poured from the open wound on her forehead. As Benny neared closer to her, he grabbed her by her hair...

"I am going to rip your head clean off your shoulders."

As Benny spoke, Lauren closed her eyes, she was shaking so hard that her teeth were chattering. She could feel his grip on her hair getting tighter as he started to pull. Every memory Lauren had, locked up in her subconscious mind, came flooding out in a flashback movie. There was so much she wanted to do with Jared, so many things she wanted to say to him. So many lost years with her father. Lauren had been so close to getting the answers she had longingly sought after. So much of her life had been secrets and lies, now any chances of redemption were on the verge of extinction.

"Benny let her go!"

Lauren opened her eyes. It was Zenon, he was standing behind Benny.

"Please don't kill your own cousin."

Lauren and Benny were both confused by Zenon's words, cousin? They couldn't possibly be related. Benny let go of Lauren and turned towards Zenon. His eyes were glistening green, his stare was intense and frightening, there was extraordinary power inside of Benny, power that he didn't even know he had, but Zenon could see it, radiating from Benny's soul through his eyes. Benny moved closer to Zenon, demanding the elder to explain himself.

Lauren could now see the power emancipating from Benny's shirtless body.

"You have no idea where you came from because Kais has never wanted you to know." Zenon edged closer to Benny, who was intrigued to hear what Zenon had to say.

"I am a Kane now!"

Benny snarled at Zenon.

"Yes, you are a Kane, but you are also a Valentin."

Zenon went on to tell Benny that his mother was Maya Kane, the sister of Kais Kane, the sister he killed years before but never told anyone why.

"You see Benny, Maya fell in love with my brother, Charles Valentin, a blue blood elf.

As you can imagine, this infuriated a lot of people. An elf and a fairy are sworn enemies.

Your parents believed their love for one another would unite the two creatures and bring peace. Your mother was bad and your father was good, but somehow, they balanced each other perfectly, in a way that no one has ever even dared to imagine before. Kais would not except this relationship and forbade your mother to see Charles again. Your parents went on the run for five years, they changed their identities, the way they looked and their surname to Ward; they hid so they could be together. When Kais finally caught up with them, he had found that they'd had you - the first ever fairy/elf hybrid. You are the only one of your kind, Benny, there is no other like you in existence. Kais murdered them both when you were a small child. The Kane's are your family, but so are we!"

Benny was confused, he accused Zenon of lying just to try and save this daughter. Zenon told Benny that being an elf and a fairy meant he was more powerful than any other creature: that Kais knew this and wanted to keep him from ever knowing the truth, "He knew you would make the perfect warrior for his army."

Zenon then went on to tell him that no one knew he even existed until after the fairies were imprisoned in Fey Forest. They found a letter in Kais' belongings from Charles Valentin to Zenon, telling him that Benny had been born. The letter never arrived because Kais killed them before it was sent.

The prophecy of Lauren being the end of the good world or the start of an evil one, was always presumed that it would be a choice that she makes. But the truth is, her death or survival at the hands of Benny, is truly where the legend starts and finishes. He told Benny that by killing Lauren, he would be burning the bridge of any future peace between good and bad.

"You would have chosen the dark side in which there would be no return."

Zenon told Benny, that if he chose to kill Lauren today in these woods, then everything his parents fought and died for, would have been for nothing.

"Benny, you were the symbol of hope. You are the future."

Benny turned to look at Lauren who had now managed to stand up. He and Lauren were the same, they had both spent their lives trying to find out where they come from and now the reality of knowing the truth was too much to handle. Benny ran off into the woods without saying a word.

Zenon rushed over to his daughter and placed his hand over her wound. He closed his eyes and within seconds the gash on her forehead that was pouring with blood, had completely healed. Lauren put her arms around her father and hugged him tightly.

Moments ago, she thought she was about to take her finals breaths on earth, but here she stood, alive and well and still in the thick of a battle between mythical creatures.

Zenon led Lauren to the Safe Haven.

As they walked, Lauren asked him why her mother couldn't remember who he was.

He told her that he had taken her memories so that she wouldn't try to come back to Eden. He needed her to take Lauren someplace far away for both of their safety.

He explained that even though many others thought that she would be the end of the good world, he never believed it. He assured Lauren that wasn't why he sent them away. He knew that, as a family, they would be stronger together than apart, but then; The fairies killed Nicole's parents in front of her, she was forced to stand and watch her mother and father burn to death in their car and she was helpless to save them, and even though Zenon tried to comfort her, she was inconsolable. It crushed him to see what his world was doing to her, so he wiped her memory and sent her off with Lauren in tow.

Zenon knew that Nicole would not go willingly. He wanted her to have a good life and believed she would find it without him.

Lauren told her father that her mother had never truly been happy, she always felt that her mother was missing something from her life. Now she knew what it was. She was missing true love. Lauren was angry with her father, she told him that he didn't have the right to take someone's choice away like that. She loved Jared and couldn't imagine having something cruel like that done to her. A world without Jared would be no world at all.

Lauren then asked her father, why he had never visited or contacted, surely, he could drop by and pretend to be a salesman or something. Just to check they were ok.

"That's the thing about true love Lauren, its stronger than any magic. Your mother would only need to take one look at me and the spell would come undone."

Zenon knew that he had made the wrong decision 18 years ago, but at the time, he thought it would be the only option. Lauren cried, she cried for her mother. Loving someone unconditionally is the most wonderful feeling in the world, sure it can be painful too, but it's an unexplainable feeling to experience.

True love isn't easy to come by and to have it taken away, the memories and the feelings and then have to live your life feeling like something is missing. It was selfish of Zenon to do such a thing. Knowing this meant Lauren understood her mother and why she was the way she was. She told her father that once this was over, he was to go to her and make things right.

CHAPTER TWENTY-TWO

Kais had called for the fairies to go back to their base, they were out-numbered and with Benny disappearing, they had no choice but to retreat. They had massacred many, but they knew they wouldn't win tonight.

Amara had fled the battle to find Daniel. Kais was furious with her for leaving when he needed her to fight. He had no idea where Benny had gone, he needed Benny more than anyone as he was the strongest of his army.

Of course, he did not know what Benny had been told earlier in the evening, so he ordered some fairies to go out and look for him and to search for Amara, too. They were instructed to bring both back to him immediately.

The elders left Eden after burning the whole town to the ground. They made it look like a gas leak explosion. It was the only way they could hide the death of so many humans from the rest of the world, without arousing suspicion.

~

Amara stood outside the house that Daniel Evans had lived in eighteen years ago. She suddenly felt anxious; what if her father was right, what if he had forgotten all about her, did he even live here anymore? What if she knocked on the front door and his beautiful wife opened the door? Amara stood outside for over an hour, contemplating whether she should knock or run or both.

Just standing outside a house in the suburbs for an hour was enough to arouse the neighbour's suspicions. An elderly man from the bungalow across the road, came out of his home and tapped Amara on the shoulder. She had been deep in thought and he startled her.

As she turned around she saw that the old man was Daniels father.

"Mr Evans, you made me jump."

The elderly man looked shocked, "Amara, is that you, why you haven't aged a day!"

Amara gave Mr Evans a hug, she was so happy to see that he was still alive and well.

"Are you here to see Daniel?"

Mr Evans spoke tenderly as his voice shook, "because he isn't home yet, my dear."

Daniel's father invited Amara to wait in his bungalow for Daniel to return from work. Amara was saddened to hear that Mrs Evans had died a few years ago.

"She was a wonderful woman, Mr Evans, I am terribly sorry for your loss."

The old man smiled and thanked Amara, he then asked her if Daniel knew she was coming?

"No, I didn't even know I was coming, till I found myself outside his old house, does he live there with his family now?"

Amara anxiously questioned.

Mr Evans chuckled to himself, "No, my dear, he brought the house from me, so that we could buy this old bungalow, he lives there alone."

Mr Evans paused as he passed a cup of tea to Amara.

"I know he will be so happy to see you, he has waited so long for you to return."

Mr Evans smiled sweetly at Amara as he sat down in his armchair. Amara felt a huge weight lift from her shoulders. She wanted so much to hold him in her arms, should he have had a wife, that desire would never have been possible.

Amara was curious, so she asked Mr Evans, "How much do you know about me?"

He told Amara that Daniel had been distraught when Amara had disappeared, his parents thought he was losing his mind as he kept saying she was being held hostage in Fey Forest.

"We contacted the sheriff in Eden and he assured us that no one was on that island. I didn't know what had happened to you, but I never believed my son was crazy. You always seemed different to us Amara, our son believed you were magical and I didn't doubt his word for a second."

Amara sat with her head bowed over, Daniel had to go through so much pain and suffering because of her and his sweet and loving parents never gave up on him.

A car door slammed shut outside. Amara leaped up and hurried over to the window. The whole world around Amara completely switched off. There he was, Daniel Evans, walking over the road towards his father's house. He had aged and changed so much but he still had the same innocent eyes, she recognised them immediately. Daniel was 5ft 9, with broad shoulders. He had put on some extra pounds over the years and his hair had started to grey on the sides. Amara still found herself attracted to him, love never changes its feelings because what the eye sees changes. No, he was still a hunk to her, just a slightly older one.

"Daniel always call in here first, on his way home from work, you wait in here my dear and I will let him in."

Mr Evans made his way to the front door as Amara stood in the lounge, nervously pulling at her sleeves.

"Hey Dad!"

Daniel sounded different, more mature, Amara thought to herself.

"Hello son, there is someone here to see you." Mr Evans ushered his son into the front room. When Daniel saw Amara, his face dropped. He was stood with his mouth open, just staring at her. It looked as though he had seen a ghost. Amara rushed over to him a flung her arms around his neck. Daniel put his arms around Amara and held her tightly. He had waited 18 years to see her again, "I knew you would find a way back to me, I knew it."

Daniel kissed her over and over again as the reunited lovers cried into one another's embrace.

Amara and Daniel decided to go for a walk, as they strolled along the path, they talked about what they had been doing. Amara was keen to hear about Daniels life and what he did for work. Daniel had been sacked from the car garage where he worked shortly after Amara's imprisonment, after a couple for years, going from job to job, he finally got his act together and started his own construction company.

He was doing really well, which made Amara proud. They had just started to talk about where their future together would take them, when a shiny black SUV pulled up next to them and three big strong men got out and grabbed Daniel, Amara went to attack, but standing behind her was a powerful witch, as the woman chanted, Amara fell to her knees, holding her head in pain. They were bundled into the car and the vehicle sped off, back towards Eden.

~

The elves were seeking refuge in the Safe Haven, whilst the other surviving mythical creatures went off to make new homes in other towns. The elves had come together and formed a wreath of shelter.

Only elves could enter The Safe Haven, but there was an ancient ritual, called The Wreath of Shelter, which allowed the gates of the haven to be opened to any creature with good intentions. It was rarely needed but today called for the doors to be opened, to keep the likes of Kymmie, Benny and Aunt Jen and Nicole safe.

The ritual required 99 elves and the chosen elder, to stand in circle around Nevaeh's Willow tree. Each elf had to hold onto a Yuhua Stone and in unison, had to cast a binding of energy spell. Once the spell was cast, the elves would place the stone on the floor by their feet and the spell would remain until the circle was broken. The lake that sat behind the magic school in The Safe Haven was lined with hundreds of Yuhua Stones.

Legend had said that, many, many years ago, there lived a young woman called Mirielle, she was half elf and half nymph. Her mother was an elf and had gone into labour in The Safe Haven, meaning Mirielle was born at the waters edge, which made The Safe Haven, the land in which she was bound too. Nevaeh not wanting a family to be separated, sent a gift to earth for her children to allow Mirielle's father, a nymph, to be able to live with his daughter inside the barrier. Nevaeh had sent a rain of beautiful flowers from the sky and as the flowers landed on the ground by the lake, they turned into beautiful rainbow coloured stones; Yuhua Stones.

The spell was created to enable creatures to come together in times of need. As long as the stones remained in a circle around the Willow tree, the spell would be active and the humans and other creatures would be safe inside.

~

Of the three hundred fairies that had come out of hiding to join forces with Kais, only 186 made it through the battle on this cold and wet night in Eden. Kais had many human witches join him in combat, most of which had also died in the fight.

The fairies were now back on Fey Forest, camps were set up all around as the Witches and fairies nursed their wounds and gathered their strength. Kais could see from his tree house window, the town that was once Eden, the whole area was engulfed in flames. One of his loyal followers stood at the doorway, "My lord, they have Amara and her boyfriend, the roads are blocked because of the fire, so they are bringing them in through the woods on foot."

Kais continued to stare out of the window, as he waved the young fairy out of the room. Amara had betrayed him, she was now going to pay for her actions.

Freja was in her tree house, looking at the piece of paper which had the spell to raise the dead, she was making a list of all the things she needed. Most would be easy enough to find, but there was one thing on the list that concerned Freja.

She needed a candle made from a special wax that you could only get from a Poppy Bee.

They were an extremely rare breed, named after the Poppy flower. These unusual Bees were bright red with yellow stripes, they only collected the pollen from a Poppy or a Rose and unfortunately, there were only two places that Freja knew off, where a Poppy Bee could be found.

Years ago, they used to be seen all over the meadows in The Valley of Anton, Freja was unsure as to whether they could still be found there. Most wildlife, plants and creatures died when the magic left the land.

The other place, that Freja knew for sure had Poppy Bees, was a place she would never be able to get too.

The Safe Haven.

The fairies that Kais had sent to retrieve Amara and Daniel had returned, the ones who went out to look for Benny hadn't been seen or heard from in a few hours.

Kais wanted to punish Amara for her betrayal, he was so angry, not only with her but also because he was losing the war with the elders. He had such a temper which he had always struggled to control.

Amara could see that he was livid with her, she rushed towards him and apologised over and over, "Please father, I love him, you have to understand. I am sorry for leaving you, please don't hurt him, I beg you."

Amara was bowed at his feet, literally begging for him to spare them. Kais pushed Amara out of his way, she fell to the ground, he walked up to Daniel and stood before him, Daniel didn't say a word, he didn't beg for his life, nor did he apologise to Kais, maybe if he had, things would have been different, but then, maybe they wouldn't have.

As fast as lightening, Kais reached forward and put his hand through Daniels chest, he ripped out his heart and threw it on the ground next to Amara.

Amara screamed as she saw her beloved fall to the floor. The tears on her cheek, immediately turned black and had almost doubled in size. She struggled to breathe. Freja looked up at her father, she could feel the power being sucked from her body and she had no way of stopping it. Amara's scars continued to grow until the teardrops burst and Amaras body convulsed. It was almost like a bomb had exploded in her brain. She was dead.

"Daddy, no!"

Freja fell to her knees, looking down at her powerless hands. Kais had become so blinded by anger that it had not occurred to him, that by killing Daniel and hurting Amara, what he had also done was drain Freja of her power.

He had not intentionally meant to punish Freja as well, he needed her on his side, he couldn't afford to lose Freja as soldier: she was strong and loyal to him.

Realising what he had done, he let out an almighty roar of anger and shouted.

"FIND BENNY NOW!"

Without Freja, Kais was now relying on Benny to help him kill Zenon and the other elders.

Kais had made a mistake, but he didn't try to comfort his daughter, he just walked past her and left her to sob in the dirt all alone.

~

Word had reached the Safe Haven that Benny hadn't returned to Kais and that he had killed the fairies that had been sent to find him.

The elves had ordered everyone to stay inside as Benny would be unpredictable and so it would be unsafe for anyone to go after him.

But Lauren was worried about him; she knew what it felt like to be told the truths of her heritage and she knew that he would be feeling very alone and confused. She decided to sneak out of the Safe Haven by herself to try and find him.

Lauren's strength was her kindness, and it was also her weakness. But he was her family too and she just wanted to make sure he was OK.

Lauren headed off into the woods with a torch, she had no clue where to look but she knew she had to try.

"Benny, where are you."

She repeatedly whispered as she wandered through the trees and into eerie darkness. Lauren was afraid, a part of her was starting to regret leaving the only place in the world, where she would be safe. But she also knew that for once in her life she was doing what she knew in her heart of hearts was the right thing and the danger of it did not scare her. If she died tonight, then at least she would die knowing she followed her heart.

"Benny."

She called for him again.

Lauren was now deep into the woods, far from safety and she could not see anything, it started to rain again, she could smell the wet grass and mud all around her. She heard a noise, it came from behind, Lauren spun around.

"You're either really brave or really stupid coming out here alone."

It was Benny, he looked like a broken and desperate man. Lauren wasn't sure if she was relieved that it was him or whether she should be worried for her life again.

"Look, you can kill me if you want, right here, right now. But I just wanted to make sure you were ok."

Lauren said as she wiped the rain from her forehead.

Lauren told Benny about how she found out being a changeling and that she had been lied to her whole life. She said that she didn't care what side he would chose, as long as he didn't make the decision thinking he was alone.

Benny started to relax as he sat down on a fallen branch. Lauren plonked herself down beside him, neither of them spoke at first, they just quietly sat in the pouring rain.

Lauren soon broke the silence between them. She told Benny about Bray and Jared, she told him about her mum and Dale and that tonight was the first time she had ever met her father. She too was still trying to process all this information.

"If I am completely honest with myself, I don't know if I am here just to help you Benny or if I am here just to try and help myself deal with everything that has happened."

Benny appreciated that Lauren had risked her life to come and find him, but more than that, he liked the fact that she didn't lie to him, he told her that although he enjoyed some of the bad things he had done, he also felt guilty too.

He had always known that guilt wasn't a usual trait for a fairy to possess, but had never expected to hear his father was an elf. He was angry that he had been lied to and upset to know he would never meet his parents.

Benny assured Lauren that he wasn't going to hurt her as she was his family, but that Freja and Amara were also his family, so instead of running and hiding, he was going to go to Kais and ask him to stop the fighting.

Lauren put her hand on Benny's arm, she had heard already that Amara was dead and Freja powerless.

"Benny, I am so sorry but Amara is dead and Freja has no power. Kais killed Amaras love in front of her and the pain literally killed her."

Benny jumped to his feet, "No! Please not Mar, she isn't as bad as the others, she didn't deserve this!"

This news had really upset Benny deeply.

He was so angry at Kais for punishing Amara like that, his own daughter!

Even though the girls had sometimes made him feel alone, he still loved them and wanted no harm to come to them. After all, he had grown up with these girls and saw them as big sisters. Benny had doubts, maybe if he had not of ran away into the woods, then he could have been there and protected Amara, maybe he could have helped.

Then he remembered what Kais is really like, there would have been no reasoning with him.

If Kais does something, no one questions him. Benny realised that had he of been there, he probably wouldn't have stood up to him, he would have been the same loyal soldier he always was. He didn't want to be that fool anymore.

Benny knew now that he had no choice. He had to stop Kais. He had to join the elves and make his late father proud. His parents had died trying to bring peace and he knew that he needed to continue their legacy and give their deaths reason.

Lauren and Benny were soaked to the bone, so they headed back to the Safe Haven.

As they approached the entrance, Lauren wanted to warn him about the spell around it and that he may feel heat and hear high pitched sounds.

"You may feel some..."

Lauren rolled her eyes as she watched Benny walk through the entrance with no problems.

"Really?"

Lauren threw her hands up in the air as she walked in behind him.

"Nevaeh clearly has favourites!"

Lauren mumbled to herself.

Benny and Lauren were met at the entrance by Zenon.

With all the commotion going on, no one had realised that Lauren had left. No one apart from Zenon. He had seen Lauren leave and chose not to stop her. He knew that the prophecy of her and Benny had to happen, but he was confident that his daughter would be strong enough to prevail. A big part of being a strong leader, meant that sometimes, you needed to let your strongest soldiers make important decisions and being a good parent, meant letting your children choose their own path, even if their choice of road looked dangerous and uncertain.

Going out alone to find Benny was something she needed to do. Zenon had already been impressed with the courage and kindness his daughter had shown.

"Your father would be very proud of you

Benny; I am very proud of you."

Zenon put his hand on Benny's shoulder as he spoke.

He then turned to his daughter and said, "Today, you have both proved yourselves to be the true Valentin's that I and Charles had always hoped you'd be."

Benny felt something he had never felt before. He felt part of a family, maybe had Freja and Amara known the truth, if they had been told years ago, that Benny was blood related, then they may have welcomed him as their family and things might have been different.

This was different, there was a bond between Zenon, Benny and Lauren, even though they were all completely different. Benny knew he had made the right choice siding with the elves, but he was still apprehensive about meeting the others.

He worried that perhaps not all elves would welcome him with the same warmth and compassion. He feared that they would push him away and he would be back to being alone. Lauren stood by him and assured him that no matter what was to happen, she would have his back and he would never be alone.

Zenon had called for all elves to gather around Nevaeh's Willow tree. There were hundreds of elves in the Safe Haven and they were all eager to hear what Zenon had to announce. It had been a very sad day for everyone, many had lost loved ones and their homes too. They needed some comforting words from their leader, they needed to know that the fairies were going to pay for their cruel and wicked actions.

Benny felt sick to his stomach, how would they react?

Zenon stood under the tree as he addressed the crowded field.

"The fairies attacked Eden and the blood of our friends will stain their hands for eternity.

We have lost a great deal and we still stand to lose a lot more. But through our fight we have remained strong and the bravery of our fallen will remain with us always.

Something great has come to us from this devastation. Today, one of our lost sons has been returned to us."

Benny could now feel his palms getting sweaty.

"Today, the son of my late brother, Charles Valentin. The child we never got to a chance to know, has returned to us."

Zenon stepped to one side and opened his arms out to a very nervous Benny.

"I give you, my nephew – Benny Ward."

Benny who was now in full panic mode, was absolutely terrified of not knowing how they would react. He had been with the fairies for so long and in that time, had done so many awful things, how could they ever want to accept him, after knowing his past. The crowd was silent as every single elf turned to look at Benny, who now had begun to shake like a leaf.

Benny stepped forward anxiously and raised his hand to wave, and as he did, something beautiful happened, something which he had never expected.

Every single elf began to cheer.

They were roaring with celebration. Elves rushed over to him to hug him and shake his hand.

"Welcome home!"

They said. Benny could not believe that they had embraced him so lovingly and easily. He turned to Lauren, who was stood by his side, she smiled at him and said, "You're obviously the golden child, I never got a reception like this."

And with that, she gave him a wink and punched him on the arm. Benny laughed, he felt at home.

After the celebrations, had taken place, Benny turned to Zenon and asked how the elves could have forgiven him so easily for all the terrible things he had done.

Zenon told him that they had learned about him when it was too late to save him.

The day Zenon had announced to the elves that he had been born but was now a prisoner on Fey Forest, the elves cried and mourned for him. Zenon explained to Benny, that he had never been given a choice, he had never known about his parents and that he too had been a victim of the fairies.

CHAPTER TWENTY-THREE

Lauren and Jared had finally managed to be alone. They had found a secluded spot, away from the others, on the opposite side of the crystal-clear lake. The sun was now rising behind them as they sat with a cosy, fleece blanket over their shoulders. Lauren had her head resting on Jared's chest.

They barely spoke, just basking in one another's aura. They were soulmates, they did not need words to communicate. Their souls spoke to each other in a language of their own. The language of love. Since the day they had met, life had thrown many dangers and obstacles in their path and each time, they had managed to overcome them and become stronger together.

Lauren looked back on her time in Middle Keynes. She was a weak little girl, who believed she was in love with Bray. What a loser, she thought to herself.

No, Lauren knew what love was now. It was not that feeling of lust you get when your eyes see something attractive. Nor was it having something you know others would be jealous of you having. Love was unexplainable, love made you the best possible version of yourself. Jared had shone a light into the parts of Lauren which she was too afraid to face before. He had awoken her spirit and helped her to grow into the courageous and compassionate women she was today.

They both knew that the days ahead would not be easy. They would be faced with many trials but they knew they had each other to lean on.

Zenon had agreed that Lauren, Jared, Jade and Kymmie could leave the Safe Haven, to go and lay Jonty to rest. He allowed it on the condition that Benny would go with them to help protect them. Not only would Benny be able to keep them safe, but he and Jade had also been getting along quite well, so Zenon thought it would be good for Benny to get more acquainted with the youngsters.

And, even though he never admitted it, Lauren was sure he was trying to play cupid.

Kymmie was a nymph, she was one of the very few survivors of her kind that fought that night. The elves had arranged to help the nymphs with funerals of their fallen. Kymmie's grandmother was no exception.

As they were leaving to go, Luna arrived with Nicole. Lauren was happy to see her mother safe, but did not hang around to catch up with her. She knew her mother was now going to be faced with seeing her father and she was keen to give them the space they deserved. She hugged her mother and kissed her on the cheek. Nicole was confused with Lauren's behaviour, Lauren would normally be the girl who would stay with her mother after such a traumatic ordeal, but now she was watching her baby run off into the woods with friends.

Luna led Nicole to a secluded part of The Safe Haven. Nicole could see a man standing by a beautiful bed of flowers. He had his back to her. Luna ushered Nicole to go over as she walked away, leaving them alone.

Nicole began to walk closer to him; she was only a few feet away. She felt like she recognised him but she couldn't quite figure it out. There was something about the way he stood that seemed so familiar to her.

Then he turned around.

His dazzling blue eyes met hers and her jaw dropped as she started to remember.

She was swimming in his eyes and as she did, the memories flooded back to her.

The day they had met, she was trying to climb a tree to help a distressed cat. Nicole kept falling from the tree. Zenon had watched her in amusement before swooping in to save her and the cat.

The first time they made love, her body and mind had never felt so electric.

She remembered the way it felt to have his hands caress her body.

The way they would laugh together.

Every single feeling rushed through her body.

"Our wedding day!"

She cried out to him as she remembered standing at the altar in the most beautiful dress she had even worn.

Nicole cried as Zenon rushed to her and held her tightly. They wept together as they kissed. Nicole felt like a teenager again, the lost years reminded her of how in love she and Zenon were. She had never felt like that with anyone else. Standing in his embrace today, it felt as though nothing had changed. She was still madly and passionately in love with him and he with her.

Zenon apologised over and over as he kissed her lips and forehead.

She had remembered everything.

Her parent's death and fairies' wicked ways. She remembered the day he told her she had to take Lauren and leave Eden. The pain she felt deep in her heart as he told her she wouldn't remember him.

Nicole was not angry with Zenon, she understood why he did it, she was just so happy to have him close to her once again. She made him promise to never take this away from her. She told him that she would rather live a life knowing she felt this way once, than ever be forced to live a life thinking she hadn't.

Zenon and Nicole spent a few hours together, alone. They caught up on all they had missed over the years. He told Nicole that she had done an outstanding job in raising Lauren alone and that she was exactly the woman, he had hoped she would become. He assured Nicole that her sister was safe. The elves had tracked Jen down at a ranch a few hours away and that they were bringing her back to Eden as they spoke. Nicole was relieved, she had been very worried about her sister as she had passed the house which was now just ashes on the ground. Nicole joked that if she had known she was seeing him again today, she would have tried to tame her wild hair and Zenon told her that he loved her hair exactly how it was.

~

Jonty's body had been placed in an iron coffin. Kymmie and her grandmother had painted the outside with pictures that represented times in his life. That was the giant's way, they would document everything in pictures which would then be buried with them. Lauren ran her hand along the coffin, looking at the beautiful drawings that the nymphs had done.

They told the life of Jonty, tears filled her eyes. Jared put his arm around her as she said her goodbyes.

Kymmie gave a heartfelt tribute to her best friend, which left not a dry eye around. She reminisced on the good times they shared as children. She thanked Jonty for being the best friend anyone could have asked for. It was always them against the world, from pretend sword fights in the woods to that time in magic school, when they were laughed at for being an odd pairing.

"Goodbye till then, my friend," Kymmie wept as she laid a large, elegant, white lily on his coffin.

As they all stood in silence around the casket, they heard a rustling noise coming from the bushes. They all turned around, praying it wouldn't be the fairies.

They all looked at the bush as it rustled and moved around.

Suddenly a little face appeared through the green leaves. It was Darrig, Jonty's gnome.

He had been missing since Jonty had died. Kymmie had searched everywhere to try and find him but he had disappeared.

His face was a picture of fear and sadness, as he looked at coffin. He had been all alone in the woods, trying to stay hidden since Jonty's passing.

"Oh Darrig! There you are, you silly little gnome."

Kymmie rushed over and scooped him out from the bushes. She was so happy to see him. When Jonty was alive, she would moan constantly about how annoying he was, but suddenly, she had never been happier to see him. He was the last piece of Jonty she had left and vowed there and then, that she would look after him, always and forever. It is what Jonty would have wanted.

They placed Jonty's body in the ground and as they did, Jade sang a beautiful song. Benny looked on at Jade in awe as the perfectly pitched song filled the air. They had finally laid him to rest. The group of friends stood silently around his grave, tears falling from their eyes as they said goodbye to the gentle giant.

Jared took Laurens hand. She looked at him and smiled as she then reached out her other hand to Kymmie. Soon they were all stood around the casket, holding hands. They made a promise on this day to Jonty and themselves that they would look after each other and protect each other, always.

A great friendship had formed between them and nothing would ever break that from this day on.

~

Kais Kane had learnt of Benny's betrayal with the elves.

He locked himself away.

He was furious.

Everything had been going to plan. Everything had been executed perfectly up until now. He had lost Amara and Benny and now Freja was powerless. His army was unsettled and questions of the fairies' next steps were being asked.

There was a knock on his door, it was Freja. She walked into the room looking very sorry for herself.

"Stop moping girl, we have work to do."

Kais was unsympathetic to his very upset daughter. Freja was so mad at him, she was powerless because of him and now he was telling her to 'stop moping!'

"I have no powers Father! I am weak and useless; you may as well just end my life now!"

Kais told Freja to stop being dramatic, which annoyed Freja further. He clearly was not taking this seriously. Freja's plan to resurrect her beloved Makkalai was ruined. How could she raise the dead, when right now she couldn't even raise a feather from the floor! Freja had no way of protecting herself, she had caused pain and suffering to so many over the years, they would surely come gunning for revenge as soon as word was to spread of her being powerless.

"Don't fret my daughter, there is a way to get your powers back."

Kais had now moved closer to Freja.

She was confused, she had never heard of this being done before.

"How?" she asked.

Kais Kane turned to look at the ash covered town of Eden, with a devious smile on his face, he said,

"By freeing Demelza from purgatory and I know how we do it..."

To be continued...